"TO ARMS"

Bill, dressed only in natty orange underpants and boots, grabbed up an ion rifle, checked that it was fully charged, then joined the others on the porch to enjoy the fun. Explosions and screams of pain penetrated the clouds of drifting volcanic smog.

"Here that? Must of got a dozen of the bowbers that time!"

"And I almost volunteered for OCS!"

It was good, clean fun and Bill, smiling with heartfelt pleasure, wandered out onto the grass to see if he could get a better view of the entertainment....

—From "Bill, the Galactic Hero's Happy Holiday"

Plus many more galactic dreams from the imagination of Harry Harrison!

Tor books by Harry Harrison

The Hammer and the Cross
The Jupiter Plague
Montezuma's Revenge
One King's Way
One Step from Earth
Planet of No Return
Planet of the Damned
The QE2 Is Missing
Queen Victoria's Revenge
A Rebel in Time
Skyfall
Stainless Steel Visions
Stonehenge
A Transatlantic Tunnel, Hurrah!

GALACTIC
DREAMS

HARRY HARRISON

ILLUSTRATED BY
BRYN BARNARD

•

PRODUCED BY BYRON PREISS VISUAL PUBLICATIONS, INC.

A Tom Doherty Associates Book
New York

This is a work of fiction. All the characters and events portrayed in this book are fictitious, and any resemblance to real people or events is purely coincidental.

GALACTIC DREAMS

Copyright © 1994 by Harry Harrison

Cover art by Keith Parkinson
Interior illustrations by Bryn Barnard

A Tor Book
Published by Tom Doherty Associates, Inc.
175 Fifth Avenue
New York, NY 10010

Tor® is a registered trademark of Tom Doherty Associates, Inc.

ISBN: 0-812-55058-7
Library of Congress Catalog Card Number: 93-45289

First edition: April 1994
First mass market edition: May 1995

Printed in the United States of America

0 9 8 7 6 5 4 3 2 1

CONTENTS

Introduction: A Writer's Life   9

I Always Do What Teddy Says   19

Space Rats of the CCC   33

Down to Earth   53

A Criminal Act   83

Famous First Words   103

The Pad—A Story of the Day After the
    Day After Tomorrow   113

If   131

Mute Milton   143

Simulated Trainer   155

At Last, the True Story of Frankenstein   179

The Robot Who Wanted to Know   189

Bill, the Galactic Hero's Happy Holiday   201

GALACTIC
DREAMS

have recently been reading Brian W. Aldiss's autobiographical work titled *Bury My Heart at W. H. Smith's.* (Smith's is the largest chain of booksellers in Great Britain, not a bespoke graveyard, and the heart referred to is a metaphorical one.) The book wanders like a pleasant stream through green meadows—and dark woods, just as a writer's life does. People enter this life and leave; there are both good and bad times. But hovering over the physical life of its author are insubstantial spirits; the books and stories that have been summoned to life by this fascinating and talented writer. From life comes art; art becomes life.

From the outside a writer's life might appear uncommonly dull. Rise in the morning and proceed to the study. Then with pen, pencil, typewriter, computer sit like a monk in a cell for long hours. The only movement the flashing—or plodding—fingers.

But it's not like that at all. It is wildly exciting. The work on the page is reality, experience, knowledge, imagination transmogrified and transformed into art. Yes, art, the word should not be shied away from. Anyone can type "With a gentle sigh . . ." on a sheet of paper. But it ceases to be a typing exercise when supposedly wise publishers force money upon one for simply writing those words. It must be an art—a black one perhaps—that makes them do something like that.

I wrote those words in Mexico in 1956. Then in 1957 and 1958, in London, Italy and Long Island, New York, I added sixty-four thousand, nine hundred and ninety-six more words to these four. And John W. Campbell bought these words, paying three cents for each one, and published them as a serial in his magazine *Astounding Science Fiction.*

Within a year Bantam Books bought these same words again and published them as a paperback book entitled *Deathworld.* My first novel. There were more to come.

The reasons why I wrote this book are clear enough; science fiction has always been my pleasure and enthusiasm. But what on earth was I doing in Mexico? Not to mention London or Anacapri.

And thereby hangs the tale. Life becomes art; art becomes life. One shapes the other always, forcefully and immutably.

We lived in New York in an air-conditioned apartment. My wife, Joan, was a successful dancer and dress designer before devoting most of her time to the family and our son Todd and our daughter Moira. I was a successful commercial artist, art director, editor, writer.

But I was writing for money not pleasure. It was like being a prison guard or an elevator operator. You did it to stay alive, not because you enjoyed it. Only the fiction, particularly the science fiction, gave me any pleasure and sense of purpose.

But in those penny and two-cent a word days you couldn't live by writing science fiction. You would have to write—and sell!—at least two stories a week to earn as much as a shoe salesman. Impossible! As for writing a novel, earning no money at all for one or two years, that was simply out of the question. Many writers have written novels in their spare time while holding down a regular job. I could not do it. It fitted neither my temperament nor my work patterns. Joan and I discussed the problem at great length and came up with what appeared to be an obvious solution.

I would quit my job, we would give up the apartment, sell the air conditioner, put all our goods in storage—and drive to Mexico. Todd, aged one, did not seem bothered about the idea.

His grandparents thought quite differently. As did all our friends. Words like "insane" and "impossible" were muttered about and occasionally shouted aloud. Perhaps they were right.

We did it anyway. Padded the backseat of our Anglia Ford 10 to make a playpen, tied the crib to the roof, filled the trunk with our belongings—and drove south.

The funny part is that it worked. We only had a bit over $200, but that princely sum went a long way in Mexico in the fifties. We drove farther south still until the paved road ended, turned back and stopped at the first town. Cuautla, Morelos. We rented a house there, learned to speak Spanish, drank Tequila at 75 cents a liter, and employed a full-time maid at $4.53 a month. I wrote on a tiny screened balcony with a view of growing banana trees just outside. My magazine articles were selling well back in New York. The income from one sale,

that might have bought a good meal and a night in the
theater in the Apple, supported us in Mexico for a
month. Once I was ahead on article sales, some short
science fiction written and sold—I took a deep breath
and started the novel.

Mexico was warm, beautiful and comfortable. But the
social life was nonexistent and the tropics no place to
bring up a baby. So after one year, rich with experiences,
tan of skin and slightly more solvent, we drove back to
New York.

And continued on to England.

Many times many people, eyebrows raised, have asked
me why I did this or that. Like driving to Mexico with an
infant. Or going to Denmark for a one month visit and
staying for seven years. My answer, quite often, is that it
seemed like a good idea at the time. People with regular
jobs, mortgaged homes, children in school and a pension
hovering goldenly in the distance are often infuriated by
this answer.

But it is a true one, not a glib or evasive answer. We
were committed to the freelance life. And enjoyed living
someplace else. For a writer it was paradise. Learning
new languages, living in new cultures, responding to new
realities, ideas, experiences. I am more than blessed that
Joan shares my enthusiasms.

On the jacket of the German translation of one of my
novels is a German expression. It refers to me as a *Weltenbummler*. Was I being called a world bum? Not nice.
Professor T. A. Shippey, science-fiction scholar and lin-
guist, set me right. "No, not a bum, Harrison—though
others may think differently. It is an ancient and good
German term, not too different from our word 'appren-

tice.' Or better 'journeyman,' as in journeyman printer. A novice working at a skilled trade would go from workplace to workplace, learning new skills and crafts."

I think the Germans are right about me. *Weltenbummler* indeed. Everything new, different, interesting, educational becomes part of a writer's life. It is all grist for the creative mill. Many times the connection is obvious; I wrote *Captive Universe* after living in Mexico, seeing the life there in the isolated villages, discovering how these people understood their world. *In Our Hands the Stars* uses Denmark as a setting; the people, their attitude towards life, shape the structure of the novel.

Those are the obvious examples. But there are subtler threads in my writing, many times things that I am not aware of, that are pointed out by critics or friends. Or enemies? I do not wish to put down Peoria, home of that fine writer Philip José Farmer, but I do feel that there is more to the world than Peoria. I have lived for extended periods, for months and years, in a total of six countries. I have visited at least sixty more. I feel enriched by the experience. More important—I feel that my work has been enriched.

Circumstance, and residing outside my native country for some thirty-odd years, have certainly changed me. The way I think, the way I write. I am an internationalist now, feeling that no single country is better than another. Though there are certainly some that are worse. I speak Esperanto like a native, or as Damon Knight once said, "Harry speaks the worst English and the best Esperanto I have ever heard." I have traveled with this international language and made friends right around the globe.

Fragments from the traveler's life:

In Moscow, many years ago, a reader gave me one of my books in Russian. Not published, but in samizdat. That is, typed out by hand, circulated privately. Honor enough—and honor is about all an author can get out of Russia in the foreseeable future. Since the Soviets did not sign an important international copyright agreement, it is not illegal to steal foreign books and publish them there. I have recently discovered that I am the most pirated SF author in Russia. Which means the most popular foreign author. A boost for the ego; a sigh for the bank account.

Another fragment: Osaka, Japan. I was the first-ever foreign SF writer to be the Guest of Honor at a Japanese national convention. The twentieth annual convention. (Honored perhaps because I paid my own way there?) Much signing of books, signing the back of the jacket of one of the fans. Who, when he thought I wasn't looking, pressed it to his heart and raised his eyes heavenward in thanks. So much for the inscrutable Orient; a thoughtful look at the way SF readers prize this form of fiction.

Rio de Janeiro: Meeting a millionaire SF fan. Who never thought he would meet the author of some of his favorite books. Signing copies of my paperbacks— bound in leather.

Signing a copy of a Finnish translation of a book in Helsinki. And realizing I had never signed a contract for this book.

Doing the same in Germany, an ugly-looking transla- tion of *Deathworld*, retitled for some obscure Teutonic reason *Planet aus die falsch Zauberer*, or *Planet of the False Wizards*.

Gallic fragment: Joan and I having lunch in Paris with Jacques Sadoul and important French SF people.

Jacques, a camera fiend, clicking away as always. Within a month he sent a copy of his just-published French encyclopedia of science fiction, years in production. With our picture in it—looking very filled with food and wine. The book had already been printed, but not bound when we had that lunch. He saw to it that the event was immortalized in the glossy photo section that was bound in.

American fragment: Working on a screenplay in Hollywood, eating alone at an Italian restaurant and reading a book for company. A talkative headwaiter; do you like to read, sir? Asked if I was a writer—apparently the only people who can read in Hollywood—extracted a reluctant yes. Eyes glowing he asked if I might reveal my name. Reluctant revelation. But what a response! "Not Harry Harrison—world-famous science fiction author!" Moment of pure bliss for author. Only tempered slightly by the revelation that he was a true SF fan, attended conventions, etc.

Most authors are indeed reluctant to reveal their occupation to strangers. This is not from shyness—never that!—but from sad experience. (When questioned I usually say that "I'm in publishing," which is indeed true.) Science fiction fans and readers don't do it—but all mundanes do. There are two questions that are always asked. And I mean always.

1. Where do you get your ideas from?
2. Under what name do you write?

The second question is a roundabout way of saying "I never heard of you." In a fit of pique I once answered "Mark Twain." My interlocutor nodded wisely and said that, yes, he thought he had heard of me.

These are memories that I treasure. Not only for the

egoboo—an SF fan term, contraction of "ego boost"—
which is of course pleasurable. But more for the fact that
I am not writing in an ivory tower, that I am writing for
an intelligent readership that values my work, gets satisfaction from it—and is not ashamed to tell me so.

Yes, I work for money since I am a writer who likes to
eat—not to mention drink—and who enjoys fending for
his family. But once you get past the money you must
look at the fulfillment of reader satisfaction. SF writers
are incredibly lucky in their readers. They organize conventions and give feedback and moral aid when needed.
I do not envy Barbara Cartland. She may write a book
every four hours and have as much money as the late Mr.
Maxwell. But she has no BC fans as I have SF fans.

The stories in this book were written over the span of
many years. They reread well—even better once I had
taken out all errors that printers let creep into typeset
manuscripts. I admit to a certain amount of polishing; an
unkempt phrase here, a maladroit sentence there. But
nothing major; they were written to the best of my ability
the first time around.

I enjoy writing. I shall keep doing it as long as my
quavering fingers can fumble across the keyboard.

I also enjoy the awards that come with a writing career.
A few weeks ago I was in London, in a branch of the
booksellers W. H. Smith. Looking at the shelves, I discovered that I had been awarded one of the greatest
prizes in publishing—and no one had told me about it.

My name was posted on the shelf in the science fiction
section.

This is for real—like having your name on a star in the
sidewalk on Hollywood Boulevard. There are only ten

names on the SF shelves. Which means that enough people liked my books and bought my books to put me there in the top ten.

This is a prize that cannot be purchased or fought for. It is given by you, friendly reader. Thank you very much indeed.

HARRY HARRISON
DUBLIN, IRELAND

I ALWAYS
DO WHAT
TEDDY SAYS

The little boy lay sleeping. The moonlight effect of the picture-picture window threw a pale glow across his untroubled features. He had one arm clutched around his teddy bear, pulling the round face with its staring button eyes close to his own. His father, and the tall man with the black beard, tiptoed silently across the nursery to the side of the bed.

"Slip it away," the tall man said. "Then substitute the other."

"No, he would wake up and cry," Davy's father said. "Let me take care of this. I know what to do."

With gentle hands he laid the second teddy bear down next to the boy, on the other side of his head. His sleeping cherub face was framed by the wide-eared unsleeping masks of the toys. Then he carefully lifted the boy's arm from the original teddy and pulled it free. This disturbed Davy without waking him. He ground his teeth together and rolled over, clutching the substitute toy to his cheek. Within a few moments his soft breathing was regular and deep again. The boy's father raised his forefinger to his

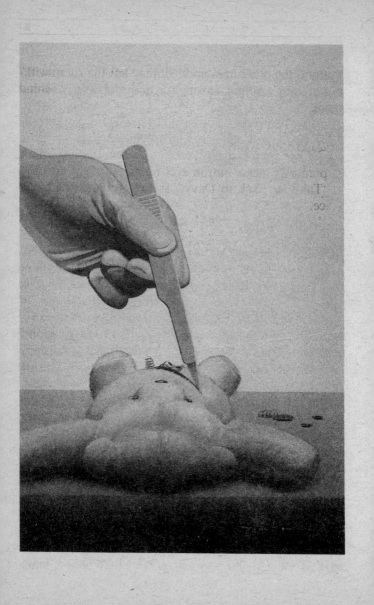

lips and the other man nodded; they left the room without making a sound, closing the door noiselessly behind
them.

"Now we begin," Torrence said, reaching out to take
the teddy bear. His lips were small and glistened redly in
the midst of his dark beard. The teddy bear twisted in his
grip and the black-button eyes rolled back and forth.

"Take me back to Davy," it said in a thin and tiny
voice.

"Let me have the thing back," the boy's father said. "It
knows me and won't complain." His name was Numen
and, like Torrence, he was a Doctor of Government.
Despite their outstanding abilities both DGs had been
made redundant, were unemployed by the present government.

They had no physical resemblance. Torrence was a
bear, though a small one, a black bear with hair sprout-
ing thickly on his knuckles, twisting out of his white cuffs
and lining his ears. His beard was full and thick rising
high up on his cheekbones and dropping low on his chest.

Where Torrence was dark Numen was fair, where
short he was tall, thick, thin. A thin bow of a man, bent
forward with a scholar's stoop and, though balding now,
his hair was still curled and blond and very much like the
golden ringlets of the boy asleep upstairs. Now he took
the toy animal and led the way to the shielded room deep
in the house where Eigg was waiting.

"Give it here—here!" Eigg snapped when they came
in, reaching for the toy. Eigg was always like that, in a
hurry, surly, square and solid with his width of jaw and
spotless white laboratory smock. But they needed him.

"Gently," Numen said, but Eigg had already pulled it from his grasp. "It won't like it, I know. . . ."

"Let me go . . . let me go . . .!" the teddy bear said with a hopeless shrill.

"It is just a machine," Eigg said coldly, putting it face down on the table and reaching for a scalpel. "You are a grown man, you should be more logical, have your emotions under greater control. You are speaking with your childhood memories, seeing your own boyhood teddy who was your friend and companion. This is only a machine." With a quick slash he opened the fabric over the seam seal and touched it: the plastic-fur back gaped open like a mouth.

"Let me go . . . let me go . . ." the teddy bear wailed while its stumpy arms and legs waved back and forth. Both of the onlookers went white.

"Must we . . .?"

"Emotions. Control them," Eigg said and probed with a screwdriver. There was a click and the toy went limp. He began to unscrew a plate in the mechanism.

Numen turned away and found that he had to touch a handkerchief to his face. Eigg was right. He was being emotional. This was just a machine. It was singularly stupid of him to get emotional over it. Particularly with what they had in mind.

"How long will it take?" He looked at his watch; it was a little past 2100.

"We have been over this before and discussing it again will not change any of the factors." Eigg's voice was distant as he removed the tiny plate and began to examine the machine's interior with a magnifying probe. "I have experimented on the two stolen teddy tapes, carefully timing myself at every step. I do not count removal or restoration of the tape, that is just a few minutes for each. The tracking and altering of the tape in both instances took me under ten hours. My best time differed from my worst time by less than fifteen minutes, which is not significant. We can therefore safely say—ahh." He was silent for a moment while he removed the capsule of the memory spools. ". . . We can safely say that this is a ten-hour operation."

"That is too long. The boy is usually awake by seven, we must have the teddy back by then. He must never suspect that it has been away."

"There is little risk, you can give him some excuse for the time. I will not rush and spoil the work. Now be silent."

The two government specialists could only sit back and watch while Eigg inserted the capsule into the bulky machine that he had assembled in the room. This was not their speciality.

"Let me go . . ." the tiny voice said from the wall speaker, then was interrupted by a burst of static. "Let me go . . . bzzzzzzt . . . no, no Davy, Mummy wouldn't like you to do that . . . fork in left, knife in right . . . if you do you'll have to wipe . . . good boy good boy good boy . . ."

The voice squeaked and whispered and went on and on, while the hours on the clock went by, one by one. Numen brought in coffee more than once. Towards dawn Torrence fell asleep up in the chair, only to awake with a guilty start. Of them all Eigg showed no strain or fatigue, working the controls with fingers regular as a metronome. The reedy voice from the capsule shrilled thinly through the night like the memory of a ghost.

"It is done," Eigg said, sealing the fabric with quick surgeon's stitches.

"Your fastest time ever," Numen sighed with relief. He glared at the nursery viewscreen that showed his son sleeping soundly, starkly clear in the harsh infrared light. "And the boy is still asleep. There will be no problem getting the teddy back to him after all. But is the tape . . .?"

"It is right, perfect, you heard that. You asked the questions and heard the answers. I have concealed all traces of my work. Unless you know what to look for in the alterations you would never find the changes. In every other way the memory and instructions are like all the others. There has just been this single change made."

"Pray God we never have to use it," Numen said.

"I did not know that you were religious," Eigg said, turning to look at him, his face expressionless. The magnifying loupe was still in his eye and it stared coldly at him. Five times the size of its fellow, a large and probing questioner.

"I'm not," Numen said, flushing.

"We must get the teddy back," Torrence broke in. "The boy just moved."

Davy was a good boy and, when he grew older, a good student in school. Even after he began classes he kept teddy around and talked to him while he did his home-work.

"How much is seven and five, teddy?"

The furry toy bear rolled its eyes and clapped stubby paws. "Davy knows . . . shouldn't ask teddy what Davy knows . . ."

"Sure I know—I just wanted to see if you did. The answer is thirteen."

"Davy . . . the answer is twelve . . . you better study harder Davy . . . that's what teddy says . . ."

"Fooled you!" Davy laughed. "Made you tell me the answer!" He was finding ways to get around the robot controls, permanently fixed to answer the question of a younger child. Teddies have the vocabulary and outlook of the very young because their job must be done during the formative years. Teddies teach diction and life history and morals and group adjustment and vocabulary and grammar and all the other things that enable men to live together as social animals. A teddy's job is done early in the most plastic stages of a child's life. By the very nature of its task its conversation must be simple and limited. But effective. By the time teddies are discarded as childish toys their job is done.

By the time Davy became David and was eighteen years old, teddy had long since been retired behind a row of books on a high shelf. He was an old friend who had outgrown his useful days. But he was still a friend and certainly couldn't be discarded. Not that David ever thought of it that way. Teddy was just teddy and that was that. The nursery was now a study, his cot a bed and with his birthday past David was packing because he was going away to the university. He was sealing his bag when the phone bleeped and he saw his father's tiny image on the screen.

"David . . ."

"What is it, Father?"

"Would you mind coming down to the library now. There is something rather important."

David squinted at the screen and noticed for the first time that his father's face had a pinched, sick look. His heart gave a quick jump.

"I'll be right down!"

Dr. Eigg was there, arms crossed and sitting almost at attention. So was Torrence, his father's oldest friend. Though no relation, David had always called him Uncle Torrence. And his father was obviously ill at ease about something. David came in, quickly conscious of all their eyes upon him as he crossed the room and took a chair. He was a lot like his father, with the same build and height. A relaxed, easy-to-know boy with very few problems in life.

"Is something wrong?" he asked.

"Not wrong, Davy," his father said. He must be upset, David thought, he hasn't called me that in years. "Or rather something is wrong, but with the state of the world, has been for a long time."

"Oh, the Panstentialists," David said, and relaxed a little. He had been hearing about the evils of Panstentialism as long as he could remember. It was just politics; he had been thinking something very personal was wrong.

"Yes Davy, I imagine you know all about them by now. When your mother and I separated, I promised to raise you to the best of my ability and I think that I have. But I am a governor and all of my friends work in government so I'm sure you have heard a lot of political talk in this house. You know our feelings and I think you should share them."

"I do—and I think I would have no matter where I grew up. Panstentialism is an oppressing philosophy and one that perpetuates itself in power."

"Exactly. And one man, Barre, is at the heart of it. He stays in the seat of power and will not relinquish it and, with the rejuvenation treatments, will be good for a hundred years more."

"Barre must go!" Eigg snapped. "For twenty-three years now he has ruled—and forbidden the continuation of my experiments. Young man, he has stopped my work for a longer time than you have been alive, do you realize that?"

David nodded, but he did not comment. What little he had read about Dr. Eigg's proposed researches into behavioral human embryology had repelled him: secretly, he was in agreement with Barre's ban on the work. But on this only. For the rest he was truly in agreement with his father. Panstentialism was a heavy and dusty hand on the world of politics—as well as the world at large.

"I'm not speaking only for myself," Numen said, his face white and strained. "But for everyone in the world, everyone who is against Barre and his philosophies. I have not held a government position for over twenty years—nor has Torrence here—but I think he'll agree that this is a small thing. If this were a service to the people we would gladly suffer it. Or if our persecution was the only negative result of Barre's evil works I would do nothing to stop him."

"I am in complete agreement." Torrence nodded.

"The fate of two men is of no importance in comparison to the fate of us all. Nor is the fate of one man."

"Exactly!" Numen sprang to his feet and began to pace agitatedly up and down the room. "If that wasn't true, wasn't the heart of the problem, I would never consider being involved. There would be no problem if Barre suffered a heart attack and fell dead tomorrow."

The three older men were all looking at David now, though he didn't know why, and he felt they were waiting for him to say something.

"Well, yes—I agree. A little coronary embolism right now would be the best thing for the world that I can think of. Barre dead would be of far greater service to mankind than Barre alive has ever been."

The silence lengthened, became embarrassing, and it was finally Eigg who broke it with his dry mechanical tones.

"We are all then in agreement that Barre's death would be of immense benefit. In that case, David, you must also agree that it would be fine if he could be . . . killed. . . ."

"Not a bad idea," David said, wondering where all this talk was going. "Though of course that is a physical impossibility. It must be centuries since the last . . . what's the word, 'murder' took place. The developmental psychology work took care of that a long time ago. As the twig is bent and all that sort of thing. Wasn't that supposed to be the discovery that finally separated man from the lower orders, the proof that we could entertain the thought of killing and discuss it, yet still be trained in our early childhood so that we would not be capable of the act. Surely, if you can believe the textbooks, the human race has progressed immeasurably since the curse of killing has been removed. Look—do you mind if I ask you what this is all about . . .?"

"Barre can be killed," Eigg said in an almost inaudible voice. "There is one man in the world who can kill him."

"Who?" David asked and in some terrible way he knew the answer even before the words came from his father's trembling lips.

"You, David . . . you. . . ."

He sat, unmoving, and his thoughts went back through the years, and a number of things that had been bothering him were now made clear. His attitudes so subtly different from his friends', and that time with the airship when one of the rotors had killed a squirrel. Little puzzling things—and sometimes worrying ones that had kept him awake long after the rest of the house was asleep. It was true, he knew it without a shadow of a doubt, and wondered why he had never realized it before. But, like a hideous statue buried in the ground beneath one's feet, it had always been there but had never been visible until he had dug down and reached it. It was visible now with all the earth scraped from its vile face, all the lineaments of evil clearly revealed.

"You want me to kill Barre?" he asked.

"You're the only one who can . . . Davy . . . and it must be done. For all these years I have hoped against hope that it would not be needed. That the . . . ability you have would not be used. But Barre lives. For all our sakes, he must die."

"There is one thing I don't understand," David said, rising and looking out the window at the familiar view of the trees and the glass canopied highway. "How was this change made? How could I miss the conditioning that is a normal part of existence in this world?"

"It was your teddy bear," Eigg explained. "It is not publicized, but the reaction to killing is established by the tapes in the machine that every child has. Later education is just reinforcement, valueless without the earlier indoctrination."

"Then my teddy . . .?"

"I altered its tapes, in just that one way, so this part of your education would be missed. Nothing else was changed."

"It was enough, Doctor." There was a coldness to his voice that had never existed before. "How is Barre supposed to be killed?"

"With this." Eigg removed a package from the table drawer and opened it.

"This is a primitive weapon removed from a museum. I have repaired it, then charged it with the projectile devices called shells." He held the sleek, ugly, black thing in his hand. "It is fully automatic in operation. When this device, the trigger, is depressed a chemical reaction propels a copper and lead weight named a bullet directly from the front orifice. The line of flight of the bullet is along an imaginary path extended from these two niches on the top of the device. The bullet of course falls by gravity. But in a minimum distance, say a meter, this fall is negligible." He put it down suddenly on the table. "It is called a gun."

David reached over slowly and picked it up. How well it fitted into his hand, sitting with such precise balance. He raised it slowly, sighted across the niches and pulled the trigger. It exploded with an immense roar and jumped in his hand. The bullet plunged into Eigg's chest just over his heart with such a great impact that the man and the chair he had been sitting in were hurled backwards to the floor. The bullet also tore a great hole in his flesh and Eigg's throat choked with blood and he died.

"David! What are you doing?" His father's voice cracked with uncomprehending horror.

David turned away from the thing on the floor, still unmoved by what he had done.

"Don't you understand, Father? Barre and his Panstentialists are indeed a terrible weight. Many suffer and freedom is abridged, and all the other things that are wrong, that we know should not be. But don't you see the difference? You yourself said that things would change after Barre's death. The world would move on. So how is his crime to be compared to the crime of bringing this back into existence?"

He shot his father quickly and efficiently before the older men could realize the import of his words and suffer with the knowledge of what was coming. Torrence screamed and ran to the door, fumbling with terrified fingers at the lock. David shot him too. But not very well since he was so far away, and the bullet lodged in his body and made him fall. David walked over and ignoring the screamings and bubbled words, took careful aim at the man's twisting head and blew out his brains.

Now the gun was heavy and he was very tired. The lift shaft took him up to his room and he had to stand on a chair to take teddy down from behind the books on the high shelf. The little furry animal sat in the middle of the large bed and rolled its eyes and wagged its stubby arms.

"Teddy," he said, "I'm going to pull up flowers from the flower bed."

"No Davy . . . pulling up flowers is naughty . . . don't pull up the flowers." The little voice squeaked and the arms waved.

"Teddy, I'm going to break a window."

"No, Davy . . . breaking windows is naughty . . . don't break any windows. . . ."

"Teddy, I'm going to kill a man."

Silence, just silence. Even the eyes and the arms were still.

The roar of the gun broke the silence and blew a ruin of gears, wires and bent metal from the back of the destroyed teddy bear.

"Teddy . . . oh, teddy . . . you should have told me," David said and dropped the gun and at last was crying.

SPACE RATS

OF THE CCC

That's it, matey, pull up a stool, sure use that one. Just dump old Phrnnx onto the floor to sleep it off. You know that Krddls can't stand to drink—much less drink flnnx, and that topped off with a smoke of the hellish krmml weed. Here, let me pour you a mug of flnnx, oops, sorry about your sleeve. When it dries you can scrape it off with a knife. Here's to your health and may your tubeliners never fail you when the kpnnz hordes are on your tail.

No, sorry, never heard your name before. Too many good men come and go, and the good ones die early, aye! Me? You never heard of me. Just call me Old Sarge—as good a name as any. Good men I say, and the best of them was—well, we'll call him Gentleman Jax. He had another name, but there's a little girl waiting on a planet I could tell you about, a little girl who's waiting and watching the shimmering trails of the deep-spacers when they come, and waiting for a man. So for her sake we'll call him Gentleman Jax, he would have liked that, and she would like that if only she knew, although she must be getting kind of gray, or bald by now, and arthritic

from all that sitting and waiting but, golly, that's another story and by Orion it's not for me to tell. That's it, help yourself, a large one. Sure the green fumes are normal for good flnnx, though you better close your eyes when you drink or you'll be blind in a week, ha-ha!, by the sacred name of the Prophet Mrddl!

Yes, I can tell what you're thinking. What's an old space rat like me doing in a dive like this out here at galaxy's end where the rim stars flicker wanly and the tired photons go slow? I'll tell you what I'm doing, getting drunker than a Planizzian pfrdffl, that's what. They say that drink has the power to dim memories and by Cygnus I have some memories that need dimming. I saw you looking at those scars on my hands. Each one is a story, matey, aye, and the scars on my back each a story and the scars on my . . . well, that's a different story. Yes, I'll tell you a story, a true one by Mrddl's holy memory, though I might change a name or two, that little girl waiting, you know.

You heard tell of the CCC? I can see by the sudden widening of your eyes and the blanching of your space-tanned skin that you have. Well, yours truly, Old Sarge here, was one of the first of the Space Rats of the CCC, and my buddy then was the man they know as Gentleman Jax. May Great Kramddl curse his name and blacken the memory of the first day when I first set eyes on him. . . .

"Graduating class . . . ten-SHUN!"

The sergeant's stentorian voice bellowed forth, cracking like a whiplash across the expectant ears of the math-

ematically aligned rows of cadets. With the harsh snap of
those fateful words a hundred and three incredibly pol-
ished bootheels crashed together with a single echoing
crunch as the eighty-seven cadets of the graduating class
snapped to steel-rigid attention. (It should be explained
that some of them were from alien worlds, different num-
bers of legs, and so on.) Not a breath was drawn, not an
eyelid twitched a thousandth of a milliliter as Colonel
von Thorax stepped forward, glaring down at them all
through the glass monocle in front of his glass eye, close-
cropped gray hair stiff as barbed wire, black uniform
faultlessly cut and smooth, a krmml-weed cigarette
clutched in the steel fingers of his prosthetic left arm,
black gloved fingers of his prosthetic right arm snapping
to hatbrim's edge in a perfect salute, motors whining
thinly in his prosthetic lungs to power the Brobdingna-
gian roar of his harshly bellowed command.

"At ease. And listen to me. You are the hand-picked
men, and hand-picked things too, of course, from all the
civilized worlds of the galaxy. Six million and forty-three
cadets entered the first year of training, and most of them
washed out in one way or another. Some could not toe
the mark. Some were expelled and shot for buggery.
Some believed the lying commie pinko crying liberal
claims that continuous war and slaughter are not necessary, and they were expelled and shot as well. One by one
the weaklings fell away through the years leaving the
hard core of the Corps—you! The Corpsmen of the first
graduating class of the CCC! Ready to spread the benefits of civilization to the stars. Ready at last to find out
what the initials CCC stand for!"

A mighty roar went up from the massed throats, a

cheer of hoarse masculine enthusiasm that echoed and boomed from the stadium walls. At a 'signal from von Thorax a switch was thrown, and a great shield of imperviumite slid into place above, sealing the stadium from prying eyes and ears and snooping spyish rays. The roaring voices roared on enthusiastically, and many an eardrum was burst that day! Yet they were stilled in an instant when the Colonel raised his hand.

"You Corpsmen will not be alone when you push the frontiers of civilization out to the barbaric stars. Oh no! You will each have a faithful companion by your side. First man, first row, step forward and meet your faithful companion!"

The called out Corpsman stepped forward a smart pace and clicked his heels sharply, said click being echoed in the clack of a thrown-wide door, and, without conscious intent, every eye in that stadium was drawn in the direction of the pitch-black doorway from which emerged . . .

How to describe it? How to describe the whirlwind that batters you, the storm that engulfs you, the spacewarp that enwarps you? It was as indescribable as any natural force!

It was a creature three meters high at the shoulders, four meters high at the ugly, drooling, tooth-clashing head, a whirlwinded, spacewarped storm that rushed forward on four piston-like legs, great-clawed feet tearing grooves in the untearable surface of the impervitium flooring. A monster born of madness and nightmares that reared up before them and bellowed forth a soul-destroying screech.

"There!" Colonel von Thorax bellowed in answer,

blood-specked spittle mottling his lips. "There is your faithful companion, the mutacamel, mutation of the noble beast of Good Old Earth, symbol and pride of the CCC, the Combat Camel Corps! Corpsman meet your camel!"

The selected Corpsman stepped forward and raised his arm in greeting to this noble beast which promptly bit the arm off. His shrill screams mingled with the barely stifled gasps of his companions who watched, with more than casual interest, as camel trainers girt with brass-buckled leather harness rushed out and beat the protesting camel with clubs back from whence it had come, while a medic clamped a tourniquet on the wounded man's stump and dragged his limp body away.

"That is your first lesson about combat camels," the Colonel cried huskily. "Never raise your arms to them. Your companion, with a newly grafted arm will, I am certain, ha-ha!, remember this little lesson. Next man, next companion!"

Again the thunder of rushing feet and the high-pitched gurgling, scream-like roar of the combat camel at full charge. This time the Corpsman kept his arm down, and the camel bit his head off.

"Can't graft on a new head I am afraid," the Colonel leered maliciously at them. "A moment of silence for our departed companion who has gone to the big rocket pad in the sky. That's enough. Ten-SHUN! You will now proceed to the camel training area where you will learn to get along with your faithful companions. Never forgetting of course that each creature has a complete set of teeth made of imperviumite, as well as razor sharp claw caps of this same substance. Dis-MISSED!"

The student barracks of the CCC was well known for its "no frills"—or rather "no coddling"—decor and comforts. The beds were impervitium slabs, no spine-sapping mattresses here!, and the sheets made of thin burlap. No blankets of course, not with the air kept at a healthy 4 degrees Centigrade. The rest of the comforts matched so that it was a great surprise to the graduates to find unaccustomed luxuries awaiting them upon their return from the ceremonies and training. There was a shade on each bare-bulbed reading light and a nice soft two-centimeter-thick pillow on every bed. Already they were reaping the benefits of all the years of labor.

Now, among all the students, the top student by far was named M——. There are some secrets that must not be told, names that are important to loved ones and neighbors. Therefore I shall draw the cloak of anonymity over the true identity of the man known as M——. Suffice to call him "Steel," for that was the nickname of someone who knew him best. "Steel," or Steel as we can call him, had at this time a roommate by the name of L——. Later, much later, he was to be called by certain people "Gentleman Jax," so for the purpose of this narrative we shall call him "Gentleman Jax" as well, or perhaps just plain "Jax." Jax was second only to Steel in scholastic and sporting attainments, and the two were the best of chums. They had been roommates for the past year and now they were back in their room with their feet up, basking in the unexpected luxury of the new furnishings, sipping decaffeinated coffee, called koffee, and smoking deeply of the school's own brand of denicotinized cigarettes, called Denikcig by the manufacturer but always referred to, humorously, by the CCC students as "gaspers" or "lungbusters."

"Throw me over a gasper, will you Jax," Steel said, from where he lolled on the bed, hands behind his head, dreaming of what was in store for him now that he would be having his own camel soon. "Ouch!" he chuckled as the pack of gaspers caught him in the eye. He drew out one of the slim white forms and tapped it on the wall to ignite it, then drew in a lungful of refreshing smoke. "I still can't believe it . . ." He smokeringed.

"Well it's true enough, by Mrddl," Jax smiled. "We're graduates. Now throw back that pack of lungbusters so I can join you in a draw or two."

Steel complied, but did it so enthusiastically that the pack hit the wall and instantly all the cigarettes ignited and the whole thing burst into flame. A glass of water doused the conflagration but, while it was still fizzling fitfully, a light flashed redly on the comscreen.

"High-priority message," Steel bit out, slamming down the actuator button. Both youths snapped to rigid attention as the screen filled with the iron visage of Colonel von Thorax.

"M——, L—— to my office on the triple." The words fell like leaden weights from his lips. What could it mean?

"What can it mean?" Jax asked as they hurtled down a dropchute at close to the speed of gravity.

"We'll find out quickly enough," Steel snapped as they drew up at the old man's door and activated the announcer button.

Moved by some hidden mechanism, the door swung wide and, not without a certain amount of trepidation, they entered. But what was this? This! The Colonel was looking at them and smiling. Unbelievable for this expression had never before been known to cross his stern face at any time.

"Make yourselves comfortable, lads," he indicated, pointing at comfortable chairs that rose out of the floor at the touch of a button. "You'll find gaspers in the arms of these servochairs. As well as Valumian wine or Snaggian beer."

"No koffee?" Jax open-mouthedly expostulated, and they all laughed.

"I don't think you really want it," the Colonel susurrated coyly through his artificial larynx. "Drink up, lads. You're Space Rats of the CCC now, and your youth is behind you. Now look at that."

That was a three-dimensional image that sprang into being in the air before them at the touch of a button, an image of a spacer like none ever seen before. She was as slender as a swordfish, fine-winged as a bird, solid as a whale, and as armed to the teeth as an alligator.

"Holy Kolon," Steel sighed in open-mouthed awe. "Now that is what I call a hunk o' rocket!"

"Some of us prefer to call it the *Indefectible*," the Colonel said, not unhumorously.

"Is that her? We heard something. . . ."

"You heard very little for we have had this baby under wraps ever since the earliest stage. She has the largest engines ever built, new improved MacPhersons[1] of the

---

[1] The MacPherson engine was first mentioned in the author's story "Rocket Rangers of the IRT" (*Spicy-Weird Stories*, 1923).

most advanced design, Kelly drive[2] gear that has been improved to where you would not recognize it in a month of Thursdays, as well as double-strength Fitzroy projectors[3] that make the old ones look like a kid's pop-gun. And I've saved the best for last. . . ."

"Nothing can be better than what you have already told us," Steel broke in.

"That's what you think!" The Colonel laughed, not unkindly, with a sound like tearing steel. "The best news is that M——, you are going to be Captain of this space-going super-dreadnought, while lucky L—— is Chief Engineer."

"Lucky L—— would be a lot happier if he were Captain instead of king of the stokehold," Jax muttered, and the other two laughed at what they thought was a joke.

"Everything is completely automated," the Colonel continued, "so it can be flown by a crew of two. But I must warn you that it has experimental gear aboard so whoever flies her has to volunteer. . . ."

"I volunteer!" Steel shouted.

"I have to go to the terlet," Jax said, rising, though he sat again instantly when the ugly blaster leaped from its holster to the Colonel's hand. "Ha-ha, just a joke. I volunteer, sure."

"I knew I could count on you lads. The CCC breeds men. Camels too, of course. So here is what you do. At

---

[2]Loyal readers first discovered the Kelly drive in the famous book *Hell Hounds of the Coal Sack Cluster* (Slimecreeper Press, Ltd., 1931), also published in German as *Teufel Nach de Knockwurst Exspres*. Translated into Italian by Re Umberto, unpublished to date.
[3]A media breakthrough was made when the Fitzroy projector first appeared in "Female Space Zombies of Venus" in 1936 in *True Story Confessions*.

0304 hours tomorrow you two in the *Indefectible* will crack ether headed out Cygnus way. In the direction of a certain planet."

"Let me guess, if I can, that is," Steel said grimly through tight-clenched teeth. "You don't mean to give us a crack at the larshnik-loaded world of Biru-2, do you?"

"I do. This is the larshniks' prime base, the seat of operation of all their drug and gambling traffic, where the white-slavers offload and the queer green is printed, site of the flnnx distilleries and lair of the pirate hordes."

"If you want action that sounds like it!" Steel grimaced.

"You are not just whistling through your back teeth," the Colonel agreed. "If I were younger and had a few less replaceable parts, this is the kind of opportunity I would leap at. . . ."

"You can be Chief Engineer," Jax hinted.

"Shut up," the Colonel implied. "Good luck, gentlemen, for the honor of the C.C.C. rides with you."

"But not the camels?" Steel asked.

"Maybe next time. There are, well, adjustment problems. We have lost four more graduates since we have been sitting here. Maybe we'll even change animals. Make it the C.D.C."

"With combat dogs?" Jax asked.

"Either that or donkeys. Or dugongs. But that is my worry, not yours. All that you guys have to do is get out there and crack Biru-2 wide open. I know you can do it."

If the stern-faced Corpsmen had any doubts, they kept them to themselves, for that is the way of the Corps. They did what had to be done and next morning, at exactly 0304:00 hours, the mighty bulk of the *Indefectible* hurled itself into space. The roaring MacPherson engines poured quintillions of ergs of energy into the reactor drive until they were safely outside of the gravity field of Earth. Jax labored over the engines, shoveling the radio-active transvestite into the gaping maw of the hungry furnace, until Steel signaled from the bridge that it was changeover time. Then they changed over to the space-eating Kelly drive. Steel jammed home the button that activated the drive and the great ship leaped starward at seven times the speed of light.[4] Since the drive was fully automatic, Jax freshened up in the fresher, while his clothes were automatically washed in the washer, then proceeded to the bridge.

"Really," Steel said, his eyebrows climbing up his fore-head. "I didn't know you went in for polkadot jock-straps."

"It was the only thing I had clean. The washer dissolved the rest of my clothes."

"Don't worry about it. It's the larshniks of Biru-2 who have to worry! We hit atmosphere in exactly seventeen minutes and I have been thinking about what to do when that happens."

"Well I certainly hope someone has! I haven't had time to draw a deep breath, much less think!"

"Don't worry, old pal, we are in this together. The way I figure it we have two choices. We can blast right in, guns roaring, or we can slip in by stealth."

---

[4]When the inventor, Patsy Kelly, was asked how ships could move at seven times the speed of light when the limiting velocity of matter, according to Einstein, was the speed of light, he responded in his droll Goidelic way, with a shrug, "Well—sure and I guess Einstein was wrong."

"Oh, you really have been thinking, haven't you."

"I'll ignore that because you are tired. Strong as we are I think the land-based batteries are stronger. So I suggest that we slip in without being noticed."

"Isn't that a little hard when you are flying in a thirty-million-ton spacer?"

"Normally, yes. But do you see this button here marked invisibility? While you were loading the fuel they explained this to me. It is a new invention, never used in action before, that will render us invisible and impervious to detection by any of their detection instruments."

"Now that's more like it. Fifteen minutes to go, we should be getting mighty close. Turn on the old invisibility ray. . . ."

"Don't!"

"Done. Now what's your problem?"

"Nothing really. Except that the experimental invisibility device is not expected to last more than fifteen minutes before it burns out."

Unhappily, this proved to be the case. One hundred miles above the barren, blasted surface of Biru-2 the good old *Indefectible* popped into existence.

In the minutest fraction of a millisecond the mighty spacesonar and super-radar had locked grimly onto the invading ship while the sublights flickered their secret signals, waiting for a correct response that would reveal the invader as one of theirs.

"I'll send a signal, stall them. These larshniks aren't too bright." Steel laughed. He thumbed on the microphone, switched to the interstellar emergency frequency, then bit out the rasping words in a sordid voice. "Agent X-9 to prime base. Had a firefight with the patrol, shot up my codebooks, but I got all the ———— ————s, ha-ha! Am coming home with a load of 800,000 long tons of the hellish krmml weed."

The larshnik response was instantaneous. From the gaping, pitted orifices of thousands of giant blaster cannon there vomited forth ravening rays of energy that strained the very fabric of space itself. These coruscating forces blasted into the impregnable screens of the old *Indefectible* which, sadly, was destined not to get much older, and instantly punched their way through and splashed coruscatingly from the very hull of the ship itself. Mere matter could not stand against such forces unlocked in the coruscating bowels of the planet itself so that the impregnable impervialite metal walls instantly vaporized into a thin gas which was, in turn, vaporized into the very electrons and protons (and neutrons too) of which it was made.

Mere flesh and blood could not stand against such forces. But in the few seconds it took the coruscating energies to eat through the force screens, hull, vaporized gas, and protons, the reckless pair of valiant Corpsmen had hurled themselves headlong into their space armor. And just in time! The ruin of the once great ship hit the atmosphere and seconds later slammed into the poison soil of Biru-2.

To the casual observer it looked like the end. The once mighty queen of the spaceways would fly no more for she now consisted of no more than two hundred pounds of smoking junk. Nor was there any sign of life from the tragic wreck to the surface crawlers who erupted from a nearby secret hatch concealed in the rock and crawled through the smoking remains with all their detectors detecting at maximum gain. Report! the radio signal wailed. No sign of life to fifteen decimal places! snapped back the cursing operator of the crawlers before he signaled them to return to base. Their metal cleats clanked viciously across the barren soil, and then they were gone. All that remained was the cooling metal wreck hissing with despair as the poison rain poured like tears upon it.

Were these two good friends dead? I thought you would never ask. Unbeknownst to the larshnik technicians, just one millisecond before the wreck struck down two massive and almost indestructible suits of space armor had been ejected by coiled steelite springs, sent flying to the very horizon where they landed behind a concealing spine of rock, which, just by chance was the spine of rock into which the secret hatch had been built that concealed the crawlway from which the surface crawlers with their detectors emerged for their fruitless search, to which they returned under control of their cursing operator, who, stoned-again with hellish krmml weed, never noticed the quick flick of the detector needles as the crawlers reentered the tunnel, this time bearing on their return journey a cargo they had not exited with as the great door slammed shut behind them.

"We've done it! We're inside their defenses," Steel rejoiced. "And no thanks to you, pushing that Mrddl-cursed invisibility button."

"Well, how was I to know?" Jax grated. "Anyways, we don't have a ship anymore but we do have the element of surprise. They don't know that we are here, but we know they are here!"

"Good thinking. Hssst!" he hissed. "Stay low, we're coming to something."

The clanking crawlers rattled into the immense chamber cut into the living stone and now filled with deadly war machines of all description. The only human there, if he could be called human, was the larshnik operator whose soiled fingertips sprang to the gun controls the instant he spotted the intruders, but he never stood a chance. Precisely aimed rays from two blasters zeroed in on him and in a millisecond he was no more than a charred fragment of smoking flesh in the chair. Corps justice was striking at last to the larshnik lair.

Justice it was, impersonal and final, impartial and murderous, for there were no "innocents" in this lair of evil. Ravening forces of civilized vengeance struck down all that crossed their path as the two chums rode a death-dealing combat gun through the corridors of infamy.

"This is the big one." Steel grimaced as they came to an immense door of gold plated impervialite before which a suicide squad committed suicide under the relentless scourge of fire. There was more feeble resistance, smokily, coruscatingly, and noisily exterminated, before this last barrier went down and they strode in triumph into the central control, now manned by a single figure at the main panel. Superlarsh himself, secret head of the empire of interstellar crime.

"You have met your destiny," Steel intoned grimly, his weapon fixed unmovingly upon the black-robed figure in the opaque space helmet. "Take off that helmet or you die upon the instant."

His only reply was a slobbered growl of inchoate rage, and for a long instant the black-gloved hands trembled over the gun controls. Then, ever so slowly, these same

hands raised themselves to clutch at the helmet, to turn
it, to lift it slowly off. . . .

"By the sacred name of the Prophet Mrddl!" the two
Corpsmen gasped in unison, struck speechless by what
they saw.

"Yes, so now you know," grated Superlarsh through
angry teeth. "But, ha-ha, I'll bet you never suspected."

"You!!" Steel insufflated, breaking the frozen silence.
"You! You!! YOU!!!"

"Yes, me, I, Colonel von Thorax, Commandant of the
CCC. You never suspected me and, ohh, how I laughed
at you all of the time."

"But . . ." Jax stammered. "Why?"

"Why? The answer is obvious to any but democratic
interstellar swine like you. The only thing the larshniks of
the galaxy had to fear was something like the CCC, a
powerful force impervious to outside bribery or sedition,
noble in the cause of righteousness. You could have
caused us trouble. Therefore we founded the CCC, and
I have long been head of both organizations. Our recruit-
ers bring in the best that the civilized planets can offer,
and I see to it that most of them are brutalized, their
morale destroyed, bodies wasted, and spirits crushed so
they are no longer a danger. Of course, a few always
make it through the course no matter how disgusting I
make it—every generation has its share of super-maso-
chists, but I see that these are taken care of pretty
quickly."

"Like being sent on suicide missions?" Steel asked
ironically.

"That's a good way."

"Like the one we were sent on—but it didn't work! Say your prayers, you filthy larshnik, for you are about to meet your maker!"

"Maker? Prayers? Are you out of your skull? All larshniks are atheists to the end. . . ."

And then it was the end, in a coruscating puff of vapor, dead with those vile words upon his lips, no less than he deserved.

"Now what?" Steel asked.

"This," Jax responded, shooting the gun from his hand and imprisoning him instantly with an unbreakable paralysis ray. "No more second best for me—stuck in the engine room with you on the bridge. This is my ball game from here on in."

"Are you mad!" Steel fluttered through paralyzed lips.

"Sane for the first time in my life. The superlarsh is dead, long live the new superlarsh. It's mine, the whole galaxy, mine."

"And what about me?"

"I should kill you, but that would be too easy. And you did share your chocolate bars with me. You will be blamed for this entire debacle. For the death of Colonel von Thorax and for the disaster here at larshnik prime base. Every man's hand will be against you, and you will be an outcast and will flee for your life to the farflung outposts of the galaxy where you will live in terror."

"Remember the chocolate bars!"

"I do. All I ever got were the stale ones. Now . . . GO!"

You want to know my name? Old Sarge is good enough. My story? Too much for your tender ears, boyo. Just top up the glasses, that's the way, and join me in a toast. At least that much for a poor old man who has seen much in this long lifetime. A toast of bad luck, bad cess I say, may Great Kramddl curse forever the man some know as Gentleman Jax. What, hungry? Not me, no, NO! Not a chocolate bar!!!!!

DOWN TO
EARTH

G ino . . . Gino . . . help me! For God's sake, do something!"

The tiny voice scratched in Gino Lombardi's earphone, weak against the background roar of solar interference. Gino lay flat in the lunar dust, half-buried by the pumice-fine stuff, arm extended and reaching far down into the cleft in the rock. Through the thick fabric of his suit he felt the edge crumbling and pulled hastily back. The dust and pieces of rock fell instantly, pulled down by the light lunar gravity, unimpeded by any trace of air. A fine mist of dust settled on Glazer's helmet below, partially obscuring his tortured face.

"Help me, Gino, get me out of here," he implored, stretching his arm up over his head.

"It's no good," Gino answered, putting as much of his weight onto the crumbling lip of rock as he dared, reaching far down. His hand was still a good yard short of the other's groping glove. "I can't reach you—and I've got nothing here I can let down for you to grab. I'm going back to the Bug."

"Don't leave . . ." Glazer called, but his voice was cut off as Gino slid back from the crevice and scrambled to his feet. Their tiny helmet radios did not have enough power to send a signal through the rock, were good only for line-of-sight communication.

Gino ran as fast as he could, long gliding jumps one after the other back towards the Bug. It did look more like a bug here, a red beetle squatting on the lunar landscape, its four spidery support legs sunk into the dust. He cursed under his breath as he ran: what a hell of an ending for the first Moon flight! A good blast-off and a perfect orbit, the first two stages had dropped on time, the lunar orbit was right, the landing had been perfect. And ten minutes after they had walked out of the Bug, Glazer had to fall into this crevice hidden under the powdery dust. To come all this way, through all the multiple hazards of space, then to fall into a hole . . . There was just no justice.

At the base of the ship Gino flexed his legs and bounded high up towards the top section of the Bug, grabbing onto the bottom of the still open door of the cabin. He had planned his moves while he ran, the magnetometer would be his best bet. Pulling it from the rack he yanked at its long cable until it came free in his hand, then turned back without wasting a second. It was a long leap back to the surface—in Earth gravitational terms—but he ignored the apparent danger and jumped, sinking knee deep in the dust when he landed. The row of scuffled tracks stretched out towards the slash of the lunar crevice: he ran all the way, chest heaving in spite of the pure oxygen he was breathing. Throwing himself flat he skidded and wriggled like a snake, back to the crumbling lip.

"Get ready, Glazer," he shouted, his head ringing inside the helmet with the captive sound of his own voice. "Grab the cable. . . ."

The crevice was empty. More of the soft rock had crumbled away and Glazer had fallen from sight.

For a long time Major Gino Lombardi lay there, flashing his light into the seemingly bottomless slash in the satellite's surface, calling on his radio with the power turned full on. His only answer was static, and gradually be became aware of the cold from the eternally chilled rocks that was seeping through the insulation of his suit. Glazer was gone, that was all there was to it.

After this Gino did everything that he was supposed to do in a methodical, disinterested way. He took rock samples, dust samples, meter readings, placed the recording instruments exactly as he had been shown, then fired the test shot in the precisely drilled hole. When this was done he gathered all the records from the instruments and went back to the Bug. When the next orbit of the *Apollo* spacecraft brought it overhead he turned on the cabin transmitter and sent up a call.

"Come in, Dan. . . . Colonel Danton Coye, can you hear me . . .?"

"Loud and clear," the speaker crackled. "Tell me you guys, how does it feel to be walking on the Moon?"

"Glazer is dead. I'm alone. I have all the data and photographs required. Permission requested to cut this stay shorter than planned. I don't think there is any need to stay down here any longer."

For long seconds there was just the crackling silence;

then Dan's voice came in, the same controlled, Texas drawl.

"Roger, Gino, stand by for computer signal. I think we can meet in the next orbit."

The moon takeoff went as smoothly as the rehearsal had gone in the mock-up back on earth; and Gino was too busy doing double duty to have time to think about what had happened. He was strapped in when the computer radio signal fired the engines that burned down into the lower portion of the Bug and lifted the upper half free, blasting it upwards the rendezvous in space with the orbiting mother ship. The joined sections of the *Apollo* came into sight and Gino realized he would pass in front of it, going too fast: he made the course corrections with a sensation of deepest depression. The computer had not allowed for the reduced mass of the lunar rocket with only one passenger aboard. After this, matching orbits was not too difficult and minutes later he crawled through the entrance of the command module and sealed it behind him. Dan Coye stayed at the controls, not saying anything until the cabin pressure had stabilized and they could remove their helmets.

"What happened down there, Gino?"

"An accident, a crack in the lunar surface, covered lightly, sealed over by dust. Glazer just . . . fell into the thing. That's all. I tried to get him out, I couldn't reach him. I went to the Bug for some wire, but when I came back he had fallen deeper . . . it was . . ."

Gino had his face buried in his hands, and even he didn't know if he was sobbing or just shaking with fatigue and strain.

"I'll tell you a secret, I'm not superstitious at all," Dan

said, reaching deep into a zippered pocket of hs pressure suit. "Everybody thinks I am, which just goes to show you how wrong everybody can be. Now I got this mascot, because all pilots are supposed to have mascots, and it makes good copy for the reporters when things are dull." He pulled the little black rubber doll from his pocket, made famous on millions of TV screens, and waved it at Gino.

"Everybody knows I always tote my little good-luck mascot with me, but nobody knows just what kind of good luck it has. Now you will find out, Major Gino Lombardi, and be privileged to share my luck. In the first place this bitty doll is not rubber, which might have a deleterious effect on the contents, but is constructed of a neutral plastic."

In spite of himself, Gino looked up as Dan grabbed the doll's head and screwed it off.

"Notice the wrist motion as I decapitate my friend, within whose bosom rests the best luck in the world, the kind that can only be brought to you by sour-mash one-hundred-and-fifty-proof bourbon. Have a slug." He reached across and handed the doll to Gino.

"Thanks, Dan." He raised the thing and squeezed, swallowing twice. He handed it back.

"Here's to a good pilot and a good guy, Eddie Glazer," Dan Coye said raising the flask, suddenly serious. "He wanted to get to the Moon and he did. It belongs to him now, all of it, by right of occupation." He squeezed the doll dry and methodically screwed the head back on and replaced it in his pocket. "Now let's see what we can do about contacting control, putting them in the picture, and start cutting an orbit back towards Earth."

Gino turned the radio on but did not send out the call yet.

While they had talked their orbit had carried them around to the other side of the Moon; its bulk effectively blocked any radio communication with Earth. They hurtled in their measured arc through the darkness and watched another sunrise over the sharp lunar peaks: then the great globe of the Earth swung into sight again. North America was clearly visible and there was no need to use repeater stations. Gino beamed the signal at Cape Canaveral and waited the two and a half seconds for his signal to be received and for the answer to come back the 480,000 miles from Earth. The seconds stretched on and on, and with a growing feeling of fear he watched the hand track slowly around the clock face.

"They don't answer. . . ."

"Interference, sunspots . . . try them again," Dan said in a suddenly strained voice.

The contol at Canaveral did not answer the next message, nor was there any response when they tried the emergency frequencies. They picked up some aircraft chatter on the higher frequencies, but no one noticed them or paid any attention to their repeated calls. They looked at the blue sphere of Earth, with horror now, and only after an hour of sweating strain would they admit that, for some unimaginable reason, they were cut off from all radio contact with it.

"Whatever happened, happened during our last orbit around the Moon. I was in contact with them while you were matching orbits," Dan said, tapping the dial of the ammeter on the radio. "There couldn't be anything wrong . . .?"

"Not at this end," Gino said firmly. "But—maybe something has happened down there."

"Could it be . . . a war?"

"It might be. But with whom and why? There's nothing unusual on the emergency frequencies and I don't think . . ."

"Look!" Dan shouted hoarsely. "The lights—where are the lights?"

In their last orbit the twinkling lights of the American cities had been seen clearly through their telescope. The entire continent was now black.

"Wait, see South America, the cities are lit up there, Gino. What could possibly have happened at home while we were in that orbit?"

"There's only one way to find out. We're going back. With or without any help from ground control."

They disconnected the lunar Bug and strapped into their acceleration couches in the command module, then fed data to the computer. Following its instructions they jockeyed the *Apollo* into the correct altitude for firing. Once more they orbited the airless satellite and at the correct instant the computer triggered the engines in the attached service module. They were heading home.

With all the negative factors taken into consideration, it was not that bad a landing. They hit the right continent and were only a few degrees off in latitude, though they entered the atmosphere earlier then they liked. Without ground control of any kind it was an almost miraculously good landing.

As the capsule screamed down through the thickening air its immense velocity was slowed and the airspeed began to indicate a reasonable figure. Far below, the ground was visible through rents in the cloud cover.

"Late afternoon," Gino said. "It will be dark soon after we hit the ground."

"At least it will still be light for awhile. We could have been landing in Beijing at midnight, so let's hear no complaints. Stand by to let go the parachutes."

The capsule jumped twice as the immense chutes boomed open. They opened their faceplates, safely back in the sea of air once more.

"Wonder what kind of reception we'll get?" Dan asked, rubbing the bristle on his big jaw.

With the sharp crack of split metal a row of holes appeared in the upper quadrant of the capsule: air whistled in, equalizing their lower pressure.

"Look!" Gino shouted, pointing at the dark shape that hurtled by outside. It was egg-shaped and stub-winged, black against the afternoon sun. Then it twisted over in a climbing turn and for a long moment its silver skin was visible to them as it arched over and came diving down. Back it came, growing instantly larger, red flames twinkling in its wing roots.

Grey haze cut off the sunlight as they fell into a cloud. Both men looked at each other: neither wanted to speak first.

"A jet," Gino finally said. "I never saw that type before."

"Neither did I, but there was something familiar . . . Look, you saw the wings didn't you? You saw . . .?"

"If you mean did I see black crosses on the wings, yes I did, but I'm not going to admit it! Or I wouldn't if it wasn't for those new air-conditioning outlets that have just been punched in our hull. Do you have any idea what all this means?"

"None. But I don't think we'll be too long finding out. Get ready for the landing, just two thousand feet to go."

The jet did not reappear. They tightened their safety harness and braced themselves for the impact. It was a bumping crash and the capsule tilted up on its side, jarring them with vibration.

"Parachute jettisons," Dan Coye ordered. "We're being dragged."

Gino had hit the triggers even as Dan spoke. The lurching stopped and the capsule slowly righted itself.

"Fresh air," Dan said and blew the charges on the port. It sprang away and thudded to the ground. As they disconnected the multiple wires and clasps of their suits hot, dry air poured in through the opening, bringing with it the dusty odor of the desert.

Dan raised his head and sniffed. "Smells like home. Let's get out of this tin box."

Colonel Danton Coye went first as befitted the commander of the First American Earth-Moon Expedition. Major Gino Lombardi followed. They stood side by side silently, with the late afternoon sun glinting on their silver suits. Around them, to the limits of vision, stretched the thin tangle of grayish desert shrub, mesquite, cactus. Nothing broke the silence nor was there any motion other than that caused by the breeze that was carrying away the cloud of dust stirred up by their landing.

"Smells good, smells like Texas," Dan said, sniffing.

"Smells awful, just makes me thirsty. But . . . Dan

. . . what happened? First we had the radio contact, then that jet . . ."

"Look, our answer is coming from over there," the big officer said, pointing at a moving column of dust rolling in from the horizon. "No point in guessing, because we are going to find out in five minutes."

It was less than that. A large, sand-colored half-track roared up, followed by two armored cars. They braked to a halt in the immense cloud of their own dust. The half-track's door slammed open and a goggled man climbed down, brushing dirt from his tight black uniform.

"Hande hoch!" he ordered waving their attention to the leveled guns on the armored cars. "Hands up and keep them that way. You are my prisoners."

They slowly raised their arms as though hypnotized, taking in every detail of his uniform. The silver lightning bolts on the lapels, the high, peaked cap—the predatory eagle clasping a swastika.

"You're—you're a German!" Gino Lombardi gasped.

"Very observant," the officer observed humorlessly. "I am Hauptmann Langenscheidt. You are my prisoners. You will obey my orders. Get into the karftwagen."

"Now, just one minute," Dan protested. "I'm Colonel Coye, USAF and I would like to know what is going on here. . . ."

"Get in," the officer ordered. He did not change his tone of voice, but he did pull his long-barreled Luger from its holster and leveled it at them.

"Come on," Gino said, putting his hand on Dan's tense shoulder. "You out-rank him, but he got there fustest with the mostest."

They climbed into the open back of the half-track and

the captain sat down facing them. Two silent soldiers
with leveled machine-pistols sat behind their backs. The
tracks clanked and they surged forward: stifling dust rose
up around them.

Gino Lombardi had trouble accepting the reality of all
this. The Moon flight, the landing, even Glazer's death he
could accept, they were things that could be understood.
But this . . .? He looked at his watch, at the number
twelve in the calendar opening.

"Just one question, Langesnscheidt," he shouted
above the roar of the engine. "Is today the twelfth of
September?"

His only answer was a stiff nod.

"And the year. Of course it is—1971?"

"Yes, of course. No more questions. You will talk to
the Oberst, not to me."

They were silent after that, trying to keep the dust out
of their eyes. A few minutes later they pulled aside and
stopped while the long, heavy form of a tank transporter
rumbled by them, going in the opposite direction. Evi-
dently the Germans wanted the capsule as well as the
men who had arrived in it. When the long vehicle had
passed the half-track ground forward again. It was growing dark when the shapes of two large tanks loomed up
ahead, cannons following them as they bounced down
the rutted track. Behind these sentries was a car park of
other vehicles, tents and the ruddy glow of gasoline fires
burning in buckets of sand. The half-track stopped
before the largest tent and at gunpoint the two astronauts
were pushed through the entrance.

An officer, his back turned to them, sat writing at a
field desk. He finished his work while they stood there,

then folded some papers and put them into a case. He turned around, a lean man with burning eyes that he kept fastened on his prisoners while the captain made a report in rapid German.

"This is most interesting, Langenscheidt, but we must not keep our guests standing. Have the orderly bring some chairs. Gentlemen permit me to introduce myself. I am Colonel Schneider, commander of the 109th Panzer division that you have been kind enough to visit. Cigarette?"

The colonel's smile just touched the corners of his mouth, then instantly vanished. He handed over a flat package of Player's cigarettes to Gino, who automatically took them. As he shook one out he saw that they were made in England, but the label was printed in German.

"And I'm sure you would like a drink of whiskey," Schneider said, flashing the artificial smile again. He placed a bottle of Ould Highlander on the table before them close enough for Gino to read the label. There was a picture of the highlander himself, complete with bagpipes and kilt, but he was saying *"Ich hatte gern etwas zu trinken* WHISKEY!"

The orderly pushed a chair against the back of Gino's leg and he collapsed gratefully into it. He sipped from the glass when it was handed to him; it was good Scotch whiskey. He drained it in a single swallow.

The orderly went out and the commanding officer settled back into his camp chair, also holding a large drink. The only reminder of their captivity was the silent form of the captain near the entrance, his hand resting on his holstered gun.

"A most interesting vehicle that you gentlemen arrived in. Our technical experts will of course examine it, but there is a question—"

"I am Colonel Danton Coye, United States Air Force, serial number . . ."

"Please, Colonel," Schneider interrupted. "We can dispense with the formalities. . . ."

"Major Giovanni Lombardi, United States Air Force," Gino broke in, then added his serial number. The German colonel flickered his smile again and sipped from his drink.

"Do not take me for a fool," he said suddenly, and for the first time the cold authority in his voice matched his grim appearance. "You will talk for the Gestapo, so you might just as well talk to me. And enough of your childish games. I know there is no American Air Force, just your Army Air Corps that has provided such fine targets for our fliers. Now—what were you doing in that device?"

"That is none of your business, Colonel," Dan snapped back in the same tones. "What I would like to know is, just what are German tanks doing in Texas?"

A roar of gunfire cut through his words, sounding not too far away. There were two heavy explosions, and distant flames lit up the entrance to the tent. Captain Langerscheidt pulled his gun and rushed out of the tent while the others leaped to their feet. There was a muffled cry outside and a man stepped in, pointing a bulky, strange-looking pistol at them. He was dressed in stained khaki and his hands and face were painted black.

"Verdamm . . ." the colonel gasped and reached for his own gun: the newcomer's pistol jumped twice and emitted two sighing sounds. The panzer officer clutched his stomach and doubled up on the floor.

"Don't just stand there gaping, boys," the intruder said. "Get moving before anyone else wanders in here." He led the way from the tent and they followed.

They slipped behind a row of parked trucks and crouched there while a squad of scuttle-helmeted soldiers ran by them towards the hammering guns. A cannon began firing and the flames started to die down. Their guide leaned back and whispered.

"That's only a diversion, just six guys and a lot a noise. Though they did get one of the fuel trucks. These krautheads are going to find this out pretty quickly and start heading back here on the double. So let's make tracks—now!"

He slipped from behind the trucks and the three of them ran into the darkness of the desert. After a few yards the astronauts were staggering, but they kept on until they almost fell into an arroyo where the black shape of a jeep was sitting. The motor started as they hauled themselves into it and, without lights, it ground up out of the ditch and bumped off through the brush.

"You're lucky I saw you come down," their guide said from the front seat. "I'm Lieutenant Reeves."

"Colonel Coye—and this is Major Lombardi. We owe you a lot of thanks, Lieutenant. When those Germans grabbed us, we found it almost impossible to believe. Where did they come from?"

"Breakthrough, just yesterday from the lines around Corpus. I been slipping along behind this division with my patrol, keeping San Antone posted on their movements. That's how come I saw your ship, or whatever it

is, dropping right down in front of their scouts. Stars and
stripes all over it. I tried to reach you first, but had to turn
back before their scout cars spotted me. But it worked
out. We grabbed the tank carrier as soon as it got dark
and two of my walking wounded are riding it back to
Cotulla where I've got some armor and transport. I set
the rest of the boys to pull that diversion and you know
the results. You Air Corps jockeys ought to watch which
way the wind is blowing or something, or you'll have all
your fancy new gadgets falling into enemy hands."

"You said the Germans are near Corpus—Corpus
Christi?" Dan asked. "What are they doing there? How
long have they been there—and where did they come
from in the first place?"

"You flyboys must sure be stationed in some really
hideaway hole," Reeves said, grunting as the jeep
bounded over a ditch. "The landings on the Texas side of
the Gulf were made over a month ago. We been holding
them but just barely. Now they're breaking out and we're
just managing to stay ahead of them." He stopped and
thought for a moment. "Maybe I better not talk to you
boys too much until we know just what you were doing
there in the first place. Sit tight and we'll have you out of
here inside of two hours."

The other jeep joined them soon after they hit a farm
road and the lieutenant murmured into the field radio it
carried. Then the two cars sped north, past a number of
tank traps and gun emplacements, until finally they
drove into the small town of Cotulla, straddling the highway south of San Antonio. They were led into the back
of the local supermarket where a command post had
been set up. There were a lot of brass and armed guards

about, and a heavy-jawed one-star general behind the desk. The atmosphere and the stares were reminiscent in many ways of the German colonel's tent.

"Who are you two, what are you doing here—and what is that thing you parachuted down in?" The general snapped the questions in a no-nonsense voice.

Dan had a lot of questions he wanted to ask first, but he knew better than to argue with a general. He told about the Moon flight, the loss of communication, and their return. Throughout the general looked at him steadily, nor did he change his expression. He did not say a word until Dan was finished. Then he spoke.

"Gentlemen, I don't know what to make of all your talk of rockets, Moon-shots, Russian sputniks or the rest. Either of you are both mad or I am, though I admit you have an impressive piece of hardware out on that tank carrier. You sound just as American as I do but what you say just doesn't make any kind of sense. I doubt if the Russians have time or resources now for rocketry, since they are slowly being pulverized and pushed back across Siberia. Every other country in Europe has fallen to the Nazis and they have brought their war to this hemisphere, have established bases in Central America, occupied Florida and made more landings along the Gulf Coast. I can't pretend to understand what is happening here so I'm sending you off to the national capitol in Denver in the morning."

In the plane next day, somewhere over the high peaks of the Rockies, they pieced together part of the puzzle. Lieutenant Reeves rode with them, ostensibly as a guide, but his pistol was handy and the holster flap loose.

"It's the same date and the same world that we left,"

Gino explained, "but a lot of things are different. Too many things. Everything seems all the same up to a point, then history begins to change radically. Reeves, didn't you tell me that President Roosevelt died during his first term?"

"Pneumonia, he never was too strong, died before he had finished a year in office. He had a lot of wild-sounding schemes but they didn't help. Vice-President Garner took over. Things just didn't seem the same when John Nance said them, not like when Roosevelt said them. There were lots of fights, trouble in Congress, the depression got worse, and the whole country didn't start getting better until about 1936, when Landon was elected. There were still a lot of people out of work, but with the war starting in Europe they were buying lots of things from us, food, machines, even guns."

"Britain and the Allies, you mean?"

"I mean everybody, Germans too. Though that made a lot of people here mad. But the policy was no-foreign-entanglements and do business with anyone who's willing to pay. It wasn't until the invasion of Britain that people began to realize that the Nazis weren't the best customers in the world, but by then it was too late."

"It's like a mirror image of the real world, a warped mirror," Dan said, drawing savagely on his cigarette. "While we were going around the Moon something happened to change the whole world to the way it would have been if history had been altered sometime in the early thirties."

"World didn't change, boys," Reeves said, "it's always been just the way it is now. Though I admit the way you tell it, it sure does sound a lot better. But it's either the whole world or you, and I'm banking on the simpler of the two. Don't know what kind of an experiment the Air Corps had you two involved in but it must have addled your gray matter.

"I can't buy that," Gino insisted. "I know I'm beginning to feel like I have lost my marbles, but whenever I do I just think about the capsule we landed in. How are you going to explain that away?"

"I'm not even going to try. I know there are a lot of gadgets and things in it that got the engineers and the university profs tearing their hair out, but that doesn't bother me. I'm going back to the shooting war where things are simpler. Until it is proved differently I think that you are both nuts, if you'll pardon the expression, sirs."

The official reaction in Denver was basically the same. A staff car, complete with MP motorcycle outriders, picked them up as soon as they had landed at Lowry Field and took them directly to Fitzsimmons Hospital. They were taken directly to the laboratories, where what must have been a good half of the giant hospital's staff took turns prodding, questioning and testing them. They were encouraged to speak many times with lie-detector instrumentation attached to them—but none of their own questions were ever answered. From time to time high-ranking officers looked on gloomily, but took no part in the examination. They talked for hours into tape recorders, answering questions about every possible field from history to physics. When they got too tired to talk they were kept going on Benzedrine. There was more than a week of this in which the two officers saw each other only by chance in the examining rooms, until they were weak from fatigue and hazy from the drugs. None of their questions were answered, they were just reassured that everything would be taken care of as soon as the examinations were over. When the interruption came it was a welcome surprise, and apparently unexpected.

Gino was being probed by a recently drafted history professor who wore oxidized captain's bars and a gravy-stained battle jacket. Since his voice was hoarse from the days of prolonged questioning, Gino held the microphone close to his mouth and talked in a whisper.

"Can you tell me who was the Secretary of the Treasury under Lincoln?" the captain asked.

"How the devil should I know? And I doubt very much if there is anyone else in this hospital who knows, besides you. And do you know?"

"Of course!"

The door burst open and a full colonel with an MP brassard looked in. A very high-ranking messenger boy: Gino was impressed.

"I've come for Major Lombardi."

"You'll have to wait," the history-captain protested, twisting his already rumpled necktie. "I've not quite finished. . . ."

"That is not important. The major is to come with me at once."

They marched silently through a number of halls until they came to a dayroom where Dan lifted one weary hand in greeting. He was sprawled deep in a chair smoking a cigar. A loudspeaker on the wall was muttering in a monotone.

"Have a cigar," Dan called out, and pushed the package across the table.

"What's the drill now?" Gino asked, biting off the end and looking for a match.

"Another conference, big brass, lots of turmoil. We'll go in in a moment as soon as some of the shouting dies down. There is a theory now as to what happened, but not much agreement on it even though Einstein himself dreamed it up. . . ."

"Einstein! But he's dead. . . ."

"Not now he isn't, I've seen him. A grand old gent of over ninety, as fragile as a stick but still going strong. He . . . say, wait, isn't that a news broadcast?"

They listened to the speaker that one of the MPs had turned up.

". . . in spite of fierce fighting the city of San Antonio is now in enemy hands. Up to an hour ago there were still reports from the surrounded Alamo, where units of the 6th Cavalry have refused to surrender, and all America has been following this second battle of the Alamo. History has repeated itself, tragically, because there now appears to be no hope that any survivors . . ."

"Will you gentlemen please follow me," a staff officer broke in, and the two astronauts climbed wearily to their feet and went out after him. He knocked at a door and opened it for them. "If you please."

"I am very happy to meet you both," Albert Einstein said, and waved them to chairs.

He sat with his back to the window, his thin, white hair catching the afternoon sunlight and making an aura about his head.

"Professor Einstein," Dan Coye said, "can you tell us what has happened? What has changed?"

"Nothing has changed, that is the important thing that

you must realize. The world is the same and you are the same, but you have—for want of a better word I must say—you have moved. I see that I am not being clear. It is easier to express in mathematics."

"Anyone who climbs into a rocket has to be a bit of a science fiction reader, and I've absorbed my quota," Dan said. "Have we got into one of those parallel worlds things they used to write about, branches of time and all that?"

"No, what you have done is not like that, though it may be a help to you to think of it that way. This is the same objective world that you left—but not the same subjective one. There is only one galaxy that we inhabit, only one universe. But our awareness of it changes many of its aspects of reality."

"You've lost me," Gino sighed.

"Let me see if I get it," Dan said. "It sounds like you are saying that things are just as we think we see them, and our thinking keeps them that way. Like that tree in the quad I remember from college."

"Again, not correct, but an approximation you may hold if it helps you to clarify your thinking. It is a phenomenon that I have long suspected, certain observations in the speed of light that might be instrumentation errors, gravitic phenomena, chemical reactions. I have suspected something, but have not known where to look. I thank you gentlemen from the bottom of my heart for giving me this opportunity at the very end of my life, for giving me the clues that may lead to a solution to this problem."

"Solution . . ." Gino's mouth opened. "Do you mean

there is a chance we can go back to the world as we knew
it?"

"Not only a chance—but the strongest possibility.
What happened to you was an accident. You were away
from the planet of your birth, away from its atmospheric
envelope and during part of your orbit, even out of sight
of it. Your sense of reality was badly strained, and your
physical reality and the reality of your mental relationship changed by the death of your comrade. All these
combined to allow you to return to a world with a
slightly different aspect of reality from the one you have
left. The historians have pinpointed the point of change.
It occurred on the seventeenth of August, 1933, the day
that President Roosevelt died of pneumonia."

"Is that why there were all those medical questions
about my childhood?" Dan asked. "I had pneumonia; I
was just a couple of months old, almost died, my mother
told me about it often enough afterwards. It could have
been about the same time. Don't tell me—I mean it isn't
possible that I lived and the president died . . . ?"

Einstein shook his head. "No, you must remember
that you both lived in the world as you knew it. The
dynamics of the relationship are far from clear, though I
do not doubt that there is some relevancy involved. But
that is not important. What is important is that I think
I have developed a way to mechanically bring about the
translation from one reality aspect to another. It will take
years to develop it to translate matter from one reality to
a different order, but it is perfected enough now, I am
sure, to return matter that has already been removed
from another order."

Gino's chair scraped back as be jumped to his feet. "Professor—am I right in saying, and I may have got you wrong, that you can take us and pop us back to where we came from?"

Einstein smiled. "Putting it as simply as you have, Major . . . the answer is yes. Arrangements are being made now to return both of you and your capsule as soon as possible. In return for which we ask you a favor."

"Anything, of course," Dan said, leaning forward.

"You will have the reality-translator machine with you, and microcopies of all our notes, theories and practical conclusions. In the world that you come from all the massive forces of technology and engineering can be summoned to solve the problem of mechanically accomplishing what you both did once by accident. You might be able to do this within months, and that is all the time that there is left."

"Exactly what do you mean?"

"We are losing the war. In spite of all the warnings that we had we were just not prepared. We thought, perhaps we just hoped, that it would never come to us. Now the Nazis are advancing on all fronts. It is only a matter of time until they win. We can still win, but only with your atom bombs."

"You don't have atomic bombs now?" Gino asked.

Einstein sat silent for a moment before he answered. "No, there was no opportunity. I have always been sure that they could be constructed, but have never put it to the test. The Germans felt the same, though at one time they even had a heavy-water project that was aimed towards controlled nuclear fission. But their military successes were so great that they abandoned it along with all other far-fetched and expensive schemes like their hollow world theory. I myself have never wanted to see this hellish thing built, and from what you have told about it, it is worse than my most terrible dream. But I must admit that I did approach the president about it, when the Nazi threat was closing in, but nothing was done. It was too expensive then. Now it is too late. But perhaps it isn't. If your America will help us, the enemy will be defeated. And after that, what a wealth of knowledge we shall have once our worlds are in contact. Will you do it?"

"Of course," Dan Coye said.

"But the brass at home will take a lot of convincing. I suggest some films be made of you and others explaining some of this. And enclose some documents, anything that will help convince them what has happened."

"I can do something better," Einstein said, taking a small bottle from a drawer of the table. "Here is a recently developed drug, and the formula, that has proved effective in arresting certain of the more violent forms of cancer. This is an example of what I mean by the profit that can accrue when our two worlds can exchange information."

Dan pocketed the precious bottle as they turned to leave. With a sense of awe they gently shook hands with the frail old man who had been dead many years in the world they knew, to which they would hopefully be soon returning.

The military moved fast. A large jet bomber was quickly converted to carry one of the American solid-fuel rocket missiles. Not yet operational, it was doubtful if they ever would be at the rate of the Nazi advance. But given an aerial boost by the bomber it could reach up out of the ionosphere carrying the payload of the Moon capsule with its two pilots. Clearing the fringes of the atmosphere was essential to the operation of the instrument that was to return them to what they could only think of as their own world. The device seemed preposterously tiny to be able to change worlds.

"Is that all there is to it?" Gino asked when they settled themselves back into the capsule.

A square case, containing records and reels of film, had been strapped between their seats. On top of it rested a small, grey metal box.

"What do you expect—an atom smasher?" Dan asked, checking out the circuits. After being stripped for examination the capsule had been restored as closely as was possible to the condition it had been in the day it had landed. They were wearing their pressure suits.

"We came here originally by accident," Dan said. "By just thinking wrong or something like that, if everything that we were told is correct."

"Don't let it bug you—I don't understand the theory any better. Forget about it for now."

"Yeah, I see what you mean. The whole crazy business may not be simple, but the mechanism doesn't have to be physically complex. All we have to do is throw the switch, right?"

"Roger. The thing is self-powered. We'll be tracked by radar, and when we hit apogee in our orbit they'll give us a signal on our usual operating frequency. We throw the switch and drop."

"Drop right back to where we came from, I hope."

"Hello there cargo," a voice crackled over the speaker. "Pilot here. We are about to take off. All set?"

"In the green, all circuits," Dan reported, and settled back.

The big bomber rumbled the length of the field and slowly pulled itself into the air, engines at full thrust to lift the weight of the rocket slung beneath its belly. The capsule was in the nose of the rocket, and all the astronauts could see was the shining skin of the mother ship. It was a rough ride.

The mathematics had indicated that probability of success would be greater over Florida and the south Atlantic, the original reentry target. This meant penetrating enemy territory. The passengers could not see the engagement being fought by the accompanying jet fighters, and the pilot of the converted bomber did not tell them. It was a fierce battle and at one point almost a lost one: only a suicidal crash by one of the escort fighters prevented an enemy jet from attacking the mother ship.

"Stand by for drop," the radio said, and a moment later there was the familiar sensation of free-fall as the rocket dropped clear of the plane. Preset controls timed the ignition and orbit. Acceleration pressed them into their couches.

A sudden return to weightlessness was accompanied by the tiny explosions as the carrying-rocket blasted free the explosive bolts that held it to the capsule. For a measureless time their inertia carried in their orbit while gravity tugged back. The radio crackled with a carrier wave, then a voice broke in.

"Be ready with the switch . . . ready to throw it . . . NOW!"

Dan slammed the switch over. Nothing appeared to have happened. Nothing they could perceive in any case.

They looked at each other silently, then at their altimeter as they dropped back towards the distant Earth.

"Get ready to open the chute," Dan said heavily, just as a roar of sound burst from the radio.

"Hello *Apollo*, is that you? This is Canaveral Control, can you hear me? Repeat—can you hear me? Can you answer . . . in heaven's name, Dan, are you there . . . are you there . . .?"

The voice was almost hysterical, bubbling over itself. Dan flipped the talk button.

"Dan Coye here—is that you, Skipper?"

"Yes but how did you get there? Where have you been since . . . Cancel, repeat cancel that last. We have you on the screen and you will touch down in the sea and we have ships standing by. . . ."

The two astronauts met each other's eyes and smiled. Gino raised his thumb up in a token of victory. They had done it. Behind the controlled voice that issued them instructions they could feel the riot that must be breaking after their unexpected arrival. To the observers on Earth, this Earth, they must have appeared to have vanished on the other side of the Moon. Then reappeared suddenly some weeks later, alive and well—long days after their oxygen and supplies should have been exhausted. There would be a lot to explain.

It was a perfect landing. The sun shone, the sea was smooth, there was scarcely any crosswind. They resurfaced within seconds and had a clear view through their port over the small waves. A cruiser was already headed their way, only a few miles off.

"It's over," Dan said with an immense sigh of relief as he unbuckled himself from the chair.

"Over!" Gino said in a choking voice. "Over? Look—just look at the flag there!"

The cruiser turned tightly, the flag on its stern standing out proudly in the clear air. The red and white stripes of Old Glory, the fifty white stars on the field of deepest blue.

And in the middle of the stars, in the center of the blue rectangle, lay a golden crown.

A CRIMINAL ACT

he first blow of the hammer shook the door in its frame. The second blow made the thin wood boom like a drum. Benedict Vernall threw the door open before a third stroke could fall and pushed the muzzle of his gun into the stomach of the man with the hammer.

"Get going. Get out of here," Benedict said, in a much shriller voice than he had planned to use.

"Don't be foolish," the bailiff said quietly, stepping aside so that the two guards behind him in the hall were clearly visible. "I am the bailiff and I am doing my duty. If I am attacked these men have orders to shoot you and everyone else in your apartment. Be intelligent. Yours is not the first case like this. Such things are planned for."

One of the guards clicked off the safety catch on his submachine gun, smirking at Benedict as he did it. Benedict let the pistol fall slowly to his side.

"Much better," the bailiff told him and struck the nail once more with the hammer so that the notice was fixed firmly to the door.

"Take that filthy thing down," Benedict said, choking over the words.

"Benedict Vernall," the bailiff said, adjusting his glasses on his nose as he read from the proclamation he had just posted. "This is to inform you that pursuant to the Criminal Birth Act of 1998 you are guilty of the crime of criminal birth and are hereby proscribed and no longer protected from bodily injury by the forces of this sovereign state. . . ."

"You're going to let some madman kill me! What kind of a dirty law is that?"

The bailiff removed his glasses and gazed coldly along his nose at Benedict. "Mr. Vernall," he said, "have the decency to accept the results of your own actions. Did you or did you not have an illegal baby?"

"Illegal, never! A harmless infant . . ."

"Do you or do you not already have the legal maximum of two children?"

"We have two, but . . ."

"You refused advice or aid from your local birth-control clinic. You expelled, with force, the birth guidance officer who called upon you. You rejected the offer of the abortion clinic . . ."

"Murderers!"

". . . and the advice of the Family Planning Board. The statutory six months have elapsed without any action on your part. You have had the three advance warnings and have ignored them. Your family still contains one consumer more than is prescribed by law, therefore the proclamation has been posted. You alone are responsible, Mr. Vernall, you can blame no one else."

"I can blame this foul law."

"It is the law of the land," the bailiff said, drawing himself up sternly. "It is not for you or me to question."

He took a whistle from his pocket and raised it to his mouth. "It is my legal duty to remind you that you still have one course open, even at this last moment, and may still avail yourself of the services of the Euthanasia Clinic."

"Go straight to hell."

"Indeed. I've been told that before." The bailiff snapped the whistle to his lips and blew a shrill blast. He almost smiled as Benedict slammed shut the apartment door.

There was an animal-throated roar from the stairwell as the policemen who were blocking it stepped aside. A knot of fiercely tangled men burst out, running and fighting at the same time. One of them surged ahead of the pack but fell as a fist caught him on the side of the head; the others trampled him underfoot. Shouting and cursing the mob came on and it looked as though it would be a draw, but a few yards short of the door one of the leaders tripped and brought two others down. A short fat man in the second rank leaped their bodies and crashed headlong into Vernall's door with such force that the ballpoint pen he extended pierced the paper of the notice and sank into the wood beneath.

"A volunteer has been selected," the bailiff shouted and the waiting police and guards closed in on the wailing men and began to force them back toward the stairs. One of the men remained behind on the floor, saliva running down his cheeks as he chewed hysterically at a strip of the threadbare carpet. Two white-garbed hospital attendants were looking out for this sort of thing and one of them jabbed the man expertly in the neck with a hypodermic needle while the other unrolled the stretcher.

Under the bailiff's watchful eye the volunteer painstakingly wrote his name in the correct space on the proclamation, then carefully put the pen back in his vest pocket.

"Very glad to accept you as a volunteer for this important public duty, Mr. . . ." The bailiff leaned forward to peer at the paper. "Mr. Mortimer," he said.

"Mortimer is my first name," the man said in a crisply dry voice as he dabbed lightly at his forehead with his breast-pocket handkerchief.

"Understandable, sir, your anonymity will be respected as is the right of all volunteers. Might I presume that you are acquainted with the rest of the regulations?"

"You may. Paragraph forty-six of the Criminal Birth Act of 1998, subsection fourteen, governing the selection of volunteers. Firstly, I have volunteered for the maximum period of twenty-four hours. Secondly, I will neither attempt nor commit violence of any form upon any other members of the public during this time, and if I do so I will be held responsible by law for all of my acts."

"Very good. But isn't there more?"

Mortimer folded the handkerchief precisely and tucked it back into his pocket. "Thirdly," he said, and patted it smooth, "I shall not be liable to prosecution by law if I take the life of the proscribed individual, one Benedict Vernall."

"Perfectly correct." The bailiff nodded and pointed to a large suitcase that a policeman had set down on the floor and was now opening. The hall had been cleared. "If you would step over here and take your choice." They both gazed down into the suitcase that was filled to overflowing with instruments of death. "I hope you also understand that your own life will be in jeopardy during this period and if you are injured or killed you will not be protected by law?"

"Don't take me for a fool," Mortimer said curtly, then pointed into the suitcase. "I want one of those concussion grenades."

"You cannot have it," the bailiff told him in a cutting voice, injured by the other's manner. There was a correct way to do these things. "Those are only for use in open districts where the innocent cannot be injured. Not in an apartment building. You have your choice of all the short-range weapons, however."

Mortimer laced his fingers together and stood with his head bowed, almost in an attitude of prayer, as he examined the contents. Machine pistols, grenades, automatics, knives, knuckle dusters, vials of acid, whips, straight razors, broken glass, poison darts, morning stars, maces, gas bombs, and tear-gas pens.

"Is there any limit?" he asked.

"Take what you feel you will need. Just remember that it must all be accounted for and returned."

"I want the Uzi machine pistol with five of the twenty-cartridge magazines, and the commando knife with the spikes on the handguard and a fountain-pen tear-gas gun."

The bailiff was making quick check marks on a mimeographed form attached to his clipboard while Mortimer spoke. "Is that all?" he asked.

Mortimer nodded and took the extended board and scrawled his name on the bottom of the sheet without examining it, then began at once to fill his pockets with the weapons and ammunition.

"Twenty-four hours," the bailiff said, looking at his watch and filling in one more space in the form. "You have until 1745 hours tomorrow."

"Get away from the door, please, Ben," Maria begged.

"Quiet," Benedict whispered, his ear pressed to the panel. "I want to hear what they are saying." His face screwed up as he struggled to understand the muffled voices. "It's no good," he said, turning away. "I can't make it out. Not that it makes any difference. I know what's happening. . . ."

"There's a man coming to kill you," Maria said in her delicate, little girl's voice. The baby started to whimper and she hugged him to her.

"Please, Maria, go back into the bathroom like we agreed. You have the bed in there, and the food, and there aren't any windows. As long as you stay along the wall away from the door nothing can possibly happen to you. Do that for me, darling, so I won't have to worry about either of you."

"Then you will be out here alone."

Benedict squared his narrow shoulders and clutched the pistol firmly: "That is where I belong, out in front, defending my family. That is as old as the history of man."

"Family," she said and looked around worriedly. "What about Matthew and Agnes?"

"They'll be all right with your mother. She promised to look after them until we got in touch with her again. You can still be there with them; I wish you would."

"No, I couldn't. I couldn't bear being anywhere else

now. And I couldn't leave the baby there; he would be so hungry." She looked down at the infant, who was still whimpering, then began to unbutton the top of her dress.

"Please, darling," Benedict said, edging back from the door. "I want you to go into the bathroom with baby and stay there. You must. He could be coming at any time now."

She reluctantly obeyed him; he stood and waited until the door had closed and he heard the lock being turned. Then he tried to force their presence from his mind because they were only a distraction that could interfere with what must be done. He had worked out the details of his plan of defense long before and he went slowly around the apartment making sure that everything was as it should be. First the front door, the only door into the apartment. It was locked and bolted and the night chain was attached. All that remained was to push the big wardrobe up against it. The killer could not enter now without a noisy struggle and if he tried Benedict would be there waiting with his gun. That took care of the door.

There were no windows in either the kitchen or the bathroom, so he could forget about these rooms. The bedroom was a possibility since its window looked out onto the fire escape, but he had a plan for this too. The window was locked and the only way it could be opened from the outside was by breaking the glass. He would hear that and would have time to push the couch in the hall up against the bedroom door. He didn't want to block it now in case he had to retreat into the bedroom himself.

Only one room remained, the living room, and this was where he was going to make his stand. There were two windows in the living room and the far one could be entered from the fire escape, as could the bedroom window. The killer might come this way. The other window could not be reached from the fire escape, though shots could still be fired through it from the windows across the court. But the corner was out of the line of fire, and this was where he would be. He had pushed the big armchair right up against the wall and, after checking once more that both windows were locked, he dropped into it.

His gun rested on his lap and was pointed at the far window by the fire escape. He would shoot if anyone tried to come through it. The other window was close by, but no harm could come that way unless he stood in front of it. The thin fabric curtains were drawn and once it was dark he would be able to see through them without being seen himself. By shifting the gun barrel a few degrees he could cover the door into the hall. If there were any disturbance at the front door he could be there in a few steps. He had done everything he could. He settled back into the chair.

Once the daylight faded the room was quite dark, yet he could see well enough by the light of the city sky which filtered in through the drawn curtains. It was very quiet and whenever he shifted position he could hear the new chair springs twang beneath him. After only a few hours he realized one slight flaw in his plan. He was thirsty.

At first he could ignore it, but by nine o'clock his mouth was as dry as cotton wool. He knew he couldn't last the night like this; it was too distracting. He should have brought a jug of water in with him. The wisest thing would be to go and get it as soon as possible, yet he did not want to leave the protection of the corner. He had heard nothing of the killer and this only made him more concerned about his unseen presence.

Then he heard Maria calling to him. Very softly at first, then louder and louder. She was worried. Was he all right? He dared not answer her, not from here. The only thing to do was to go to her, whisper through the door that everything was fine and that she should be quiet. Perhaps then she would go to sleep. And he could get some water in the kitchen and bring it back.

As quietly as he could he rose and stretched his stiff legs, keeping his eyes on the gray square of the second window. Putting the toe of one foot against the heel of the other he pulled his shoes off, then went on silent tiptoe across the room. Maria was calling louder now, rattling at the bathroom door, and he had to silence her. Why couldn't she realize the danger she was putting him in?

As he passed through the door the hall light above him came on.

"What are you doing?" he screamed at Maria who stood by the switch, blinking in the sudden glare.

"I was so worried. . . ."

The crash of breaking glass from the living room was punctuated by the hammering boom of the machine pistol. Arrows of pain tore at Benedict and he hurled himself sprawling into the hall.

"Into the bathroom!" he screamed and fired his own revolver back through the dark doorway.

He was only half aware of Maria's muffled squeal as she slammed the door and, for the moment, he forgot the pain of the wounds. There was the metallic smell of burnt gunpowder, and a blue haze hung in the air. Something scraped in the living room and he fired again into the darkness. He winced as the answering fire crashed thunder and flame toward him and the bullets tore holes in the plaster of the hall opposite the door.

The firing stopped but he kept his gun pointed as he realized that the killer's fire couldn't reach him where he lay, against the wall away from the open doorway. The man would have to come into the hall to shoot him, and if he did that Benedict would fire first and kill him. More shots slammed into the wall but he did not bother to answer them. When the silence stretched out for more than a minute he took a chance and silently broke the revolver and pulled out the empty shells, putting five cartridges in their place. There was a pool of blood under his leg.

Keeping the gun pointed at the doorway he clumsily rolled up his pants leg with his left hand, then took a quick glimpse. There was more blood running down his ankle and sopping his sock. A bullet had torn through his calf muscle and made two round, dark holes from which the thick blood pumped. It made him dizzy to look at; then he remembered and pointed the wavering pistol back at the doorway. The living room was silent. His side hurt too, but when he pulled his shirt out of his trousers and looked he realized that although this wound was painful it was not as bad as the one in his leg. A second bullet had burned along his side, glancing off the ribs and leaving a shallow wound. It wasn't bleeding badly. Something would have to be done about his leg.

"You moved fast, Benedict, I must congratulate you." Benedict's finger contracted with shock and he pumped two bullets into the room, toward the sound of the man's voice. The man laughed.

"Nerves, Benedict, nerves. Just because I am here to kill you doesn't mean that we can't talk."

"You're a filthy beast, a foul, filthy beast!" Benedict splattered the words from his lips and followed them with a string of obscenities, expressions he hadn't used or even heard since his school days. He stopped suddenly as he realized that Maria could hear him. She had never heard him curse before.

"Nerves, Benedict?" The dry laugh sounded again. "Calling me insulting names won't alter this situation."

"Why don't you leave—I won't try to stop you," Benedict said as he slowly pulled his left arm out of his shirt. "I don't want to see you or know you. Why don't you go away?"

"I'm afraid that it is not that easy, Ben. You have created this situation; in one sense you have called me here. Like a sorcerer summoning some evil genie. That's a pleasant simile, isn't it? May I introduce myself. My name is Mortimer."

"I don't want to know your name, you . . . piece of filth." Benedict half-mumbled, his attention concentrated on the silent removal of his shirt. It hung now from his right wrist and he shifted the gun to his left hand for a moment while he slipped it off. His leg throbbed with pain when he draped the shirt over the wound in his calf and he gasped, then spoke quickly to disguise the sound. "You came here because you wanted to, and I'm going to kill you for that."

"Very good, Benedict, that is much more the type of spirit I expected from you. After all, you are the closest we can come to a dedicated law-breaker these days. The antisocial individualist who stands alone, who will carry on the traditions of the Dillingers and the James Brothers. Though of course they brought death and you brought life, and your weapon is far humbler than their guns. . . ." The words ended with a dry chuckle.

"You have a warped mind, Mortimer, just what I would suspect of a man who accepts a free license to kill. You're sick."

Benedict wanted to keep the other man talking, at least for a few minutes more until he could bandage his leg. The shirt was sticky with blood and he couldn't knot it place with his left hand. "You must be sick to come here," he said. "What other reason could you possibly have?" He laid the gun down silently, then fumbled with haste to bandage the wound.

"Sickness is relative," the voice in the darkness said, "as is crime. Man invents societies and the rules of his invented societies determine the crimes. *O tempora! O mores!* Homosexuals in Periclean Greece were honored men, respected for their love. Homosexuals in industrial England were shunned and prosecuted for a criminal act. Who commits the crime—society or the man? Which of them is the criminal? You may attempt to argue a higher authority than man, but that would be on an abstract predication and what we are discussing here are realities. The law states that you are a criminal. I am here to enforce that law." The thunder of his gun added punctuation to his words, and long splinters of wood flew from the doorframe. Benedict jerked the knot tight and grabbed up his pistol again.

"Then I invoke a higher authority," he said. "Natural

law, the sanctity of life, the inviolability of marriage.
Under this authority I wed and I love, and my children
are the blessings of this union."

"Your blessings, and the blessings of the rest of mankind, are consuming this world like locusts," Mortimer
said. "But that is an observation. First I must deal with
your arguments.

"Primus. The only natural law is written in the sedi-
mentary rocks and the spectra of suns. What you call
natural law is man-made law and varies with the varieties
of religion. Argument invalid.

"Secundis. Life is prolific and today's generations
must die so that tomorrow's may live. All religions have
the faces of Janus. They frown at killing and at the same
time smile at war and capital punishment. Argument
invalid.

"Ultimus. The forms of male and female union are as
varied as the societies that harbor them. Argument invalid. Your higher authority does not apply to the world of
facts and law. Believe in it if you wish, if it gives you
satisfaction, but do not invoke it to condone your criminal acts."

"Criminal!" Benedict shouted, and fired two shots
through the doorway, then cringed as an answering
storm of bullets crackled by. Dimly, through the bathroom door, he heard the baby crying, awakened by the
noise. He dropped out the empty shells and angrily
pulled live cartridges from his pocket and jammed them
into the cylinder. "You're the criminal, who is trying to
murder me," he said. "You are the tool of the criminals
who invade my house with their unholy laws and tell me

I can have no more children. You cannot give me orders about this."

"What a fool you are," Mortimer sighed. "You are a social animal and do not hesitate to accept the benefits of your society. You accept medicine, so your children live now as they would have died in the past, and you accept a ration of food to feed them, food you do not even work for. This suits you, so you accept. But you do not accept planning for your family and you attempt to reject it. It is impossible. You must accept all or reject all. You must leave your society or abide by its rules. You eat the food, you must pay the price."

"I don't ask for more food. The baby has its mother's milk; we will share our food ration. . . ."

"Don't be fatuous. You and your irresponsible kind have filled this world to bursting with your get, and still you will not stop. You have been reasoned with railed against, cajoled, bribed and threatened, all to no avail. Now you must be stopped. You have refused all aid to prevent your bringing one more mouth into this hungry world. Since you have done so anyway, you are to be held responsible for closing another mouth and removing it from this same world. The law is a humane one, rising out of our history of individualism and the frontier spirit, and gives you a chance to defend your ideals with a gun. And your life."

"The law is not humane," Benedict said. "How can you possibly suggest that? It is harsh, cruel, and pointless."

"Quite the contrary, the system makes very good sense. Try to step outside yourself for a moment, forget your prejudices and look at the problem that faces our race. The universe is cruel but it's not ruthless. The conservation of mass is one of the universe's most firmly enforced laws. We have been insane to ignore it so long, and it is sanity that now forces us to limit the sheer mass of human flesh on this globe. Appeals to reason have never succeeded in slowing the population growth, so, with great reluctance, laws have been passed. Love, marriage, and the family are not affected up to a reasonable maximum of children. After that a man voluntarily forsakes the protection of society, and must take the consequences of his own acts. If he is insanely selfish, his death will benefit society by ridding it of his presence. If he is not insane and has determination and enough guts to win—well then he is the sort of man that society needs and he represents a noble contribution to the gene pool. Good and law-abiding citizens are not menaced by these laws."

"How dare you!" Benedict shouted. "Is a poor, helpless mother of an illegitimate baby a criminal?"

"No, only if she refuses all aid. She is even allowed a single child without endangering herself. If she persists in her folly, she must pay for her acts. There are countless frustrated women willing to volunteer for battle to even the score. They, like myself, are on the side of the law and eager to enforce it. So close my mouth, if you can, Benedict, because I look forward with pleasure to closing your incredibly selfish one."

"Madman!" Benedict hissed and felt his teeth grate together with the intensity of his passion. "Scum of society. This obscene law brings forth the insane dregs of humanity and arms them and gives them license to kill."

"It does that, and a useful device it is, too. The maladjusted expose themselves and can be watched. Better the insane killer coming publicly and boldly forth—instead of trapping and butchering your child in the park. Now he risks his life and whoever is killed serves humanity with his death."

"You admit you are a madman, a licensed killer?" Benedict started to stand but the hall began to spin dizzily and grow dark: he dropped back heavily.

"Not I," Mortimer said tonelessly. "I am a man who wishes to aid the law and wipe out your vile, proliferating kind."

"You're an invert then, hating the love of man and woman."

The only answer was a cold laugh that infuriated Benedict.

"Sick!" he screamed. "Or mad. Or sterile, incapable of fathering children of your own and hating all those who can. . . ."

"That's enough! I've talked to you far long enough, Benedict. Now I shall kill you."

Benedict could hear anger for the first time in the other's voice and knew that he had goaded the man with the prod of truth. He lay silent, sick and weak, the blood still seeping through his rough bandage and widening in a pool upon the floor. He had to save what little strength he had to aim and fire when the killer came through the doorway. Behind him he heard the almost silent opening of the bathroom door and the rustle of footsteps. He looked helplessly into Maria's tear-stained face.

"Who's there with you?" Mortimer shouted, from where he crouched behind the armchair. "I hear you whispering. If your wife is there with you, Benedict, send her away. I won't be responsible for the cow's safety. You've brought this upon yourself, Benedict, and the time has now come to pay the price of your errors, and I shall be the instrumentality of that payment."

Mortimer stood and emptied the remainder of the magazine bullets through the doorway, then pressed the button to release the magazine and hurled it after the bullets, clicking a new one instantly into place. With a quick pull he worked the slide to shove a live cartridge into the chamber and crouched, ready to attack.

This was it. He wouldn't need the knife. Walk a few feet forward. Fire through the doorway, then throw in the tear-gas pen. It would either blind the man or spoil his aim. Then walk through firing with the trigger jammed down and the bullets spraying like water and the enemy would be dead. Mortimer took a deep, shuddering breath—then stopped and gasped as Benedict's hand snaked through the doorway and felt its way up the wall.

It was so unexpected that for a moment he didn't fire and when he did fire he missed. A hand is a difficult target for an automatic weapon. The hand jerked down over the light switch and vanished as the ceiling lights came on.

Mortimer cursed and fired after the hand and fired into the wall and through the doorway, hitting nothing except insensate plaster and feeling terribly exposed beneath the glare of light.

The first shot from the pistol went unheard in the roar of his gun and he did not realize that he was under fire until the second bullet ripped into the floor close to his foot. He stopped shooting, spun around, and gaped.

On the fire escape outside the broken window stood a woman. Slight and wide-eyed and swaying as though a strong wind tore at her, she pointed the gun at him with both hands and jerked the trigger spasmodically. The bullets came close but did not hit him. In panic he pulled the machine pistol up, spraying bullets toward the window.

"Don't! I don't want to hurt you!" he shouted as he fired.

The last of his bullets hit the wall and his gun clicked and locked out of battery as the magazine emptied. He hurled the barren metal magazine away and tried to jam a full one in. The pistol banged again and the bullet hit him in the side and spun him about. When he fell the weapon fell from his hand. Benedict, who had been crawling slowly and painfully across the floor, reached him at the same moment and clutched his throat with hungry fingers.

"Don't . . ." Mortimer croaked and thrashed about. He had never learned to fight and did not know what else to do.

"Please Benedict, don't," Maria said, climbing through the window and running to them. "You're killing him."

"No—I'm not," Benedict gasped. "No strength. My fingers are too weak."

Looking up, he saw the pistol near his head and he reached and tore it from her.

"One less mouth now!" he shouted and pressed the hot muzzle against Mortimer's chest. The muffled shot tore into the man, who kicked violently once and died.

"Darling, you're all right?" Maria wailed, kneeling and clutching him to her.

"Yes . . . all right. Weak, but that's from losing the blood, I imagine. But the bleeding has stopped now. It's all over. We've won. We'll have the food ration, and they won't bother us anymore and everyone will be satisfied."

"I'm so glad," she said, and actually managed to smile through her tears. "I really didn't want to tell you before, not bother you with all this other trouble going on. But there's going to be . . ." She dropped her eyes.

"What?" he asked incredulously. "You can't possibly mean . . ."

"But I do." She patted the rounded mound of her midriff. "Aren't we lucky?"

All he could do was look up at her, his mouth wide and gaping like some helpless fish cast up upon the shore.

FAMOUS FIRST WORDS

illions of words of hatred, vitriol, and polemic have been written denigrating, berating, and castigating the late Professor Ephraim Hakachinik. I feel that the time has come when the record must be put straight. I realize that I too am risking the wrath of the so-called authorities by speaking out like this, but I have been silent too long. I must explain the truth just as my mentor explained it to me, because only the truth, lunatic as it may sound, can correct the false impressions that have become the accepted coin in reference to the professor.

Let me be frank: early in our relationship I, too, felt that the professor was, how shall we describe it, eccentric even beyond the accepted norm for the faculties of backwater universities. In appearance he was a singularly untidy man, almost hidden behind a vast mattress of tangled beard that he affected for the dual purpose of saving the trouble and the expense of shaving and of dispensing with the necessity of wearing a necktie. This duality of purpose was common to almost everything that he did. I am sure that simultaneous professorships in

both the arts and the sciences is so rare as to be almost unique—yet he occupied two chairs at Miskatonic University; those of quantum physics and conversational Indo-European. This juxtaposition of abilities undoubtedly led to the perfection of his invention and to the discovery of the techniques needed to develop its possibilities.

As a graduate student I was very close to Professor Hakachinik and was present at the very moment when the germ of an idea was planted that was to flower eventually into the tremendous growth of invention that was to be his contribution to the sum of knowledge of mankind. It was a sunny June afternoon, and I am forced to admit that I was dozing over a repetitious (begat, begat, begat) fragment of the Dead Sea Scrolls when a hoarse shout echoed from the paneled walls of the library and shocked me awake.

"Neobican!" the professor exclaimed again—he has a tendency to break into Serbo-Croatian when excited—and a third time, *"Neobican!"*

"What is wonderful, Professor?" I asked.

"Listen to this quotation, it is inspirational indeed, from Edward Gibbon; he was visiting Rome, and this is what he wrote: 'As I sat musing amidst the ruins of the Capitol, while the bare-footed friars were singing vespers in the Temple of Jupiter . . . the idea of writing the decline and fall of the city first started to my mind.'

"Isn't that incredible, my boy, simply breathtaking. A singularly important and historical beginning if I ever heard one. It all started there until, twelve years and five hundred thousand words later, racked by writer's cramp, Gibbon scribbled 'The End' and dropped his pen. *The*

History of the Decline and Fall of the Roman Empire was finished. Inspiring!"

"Inspiring?" I asked dimly, my head still rattling with begats.

"Dolt!" he snarled, and added a few imprecations in Babylonian that will not bear translation in a modern journal. "Have you no sense of perspective? Do you not see that every great event in this universe must have had some tiny beginning?"

"That's rather an obvious observation," I remarked.

"Imbecile!" he muttered through clenched teeth. "Do you not understand the grandeur of the concept! Think! The mighty redwood, reaching for the sky, so wide in the trunk that it is pierced with a tunnel for motor vehicles to be driven through; this goliath of the forest was once a struggling single-leafed shrub incapable of exercising a tree's peculiar attractions for even the most minuscule of dogs. Do you find this concept a fascinating one?"

I mumbled something incoherent to cover up the fact that I did not, and as soon as Professor Hakachinik had turned away I resumed my nap and forgot the matter completely for a number of days, until I received a message summoning me to the professor's chambers.

"Look at that," he said, pointing to what appeared to be a normal radio, housed in a crackle-gray cabinet and faced with a splendid display of knobs and dials.

"Bully," I said, with enthusiasm. "We will listen to the final game of the World Series together."

"Stumpfsinnig Schwein," he growled. "That is no ordinary radio, but is an invention of mine embodying a new concept, my Temporal Audio Psychogenetic detector, TAP for short—and 'tap' is what it does. By utilizing a

theory and technique that are so far beyond your rudimentary powers of comprehension that I will make no attempt to explain them, I have constructed my TAP to detect and amplify the voices of the past so that they can be recorded. Listen and be amazed!"

The professor switched on the device and, after a few minutes of fiddling with the dials, exacted from the loudspeaker what might be described as a human voice mouthing harsh animal sounds.

"What was that?" I asked.

"Protomandarin of the later part of the thirteenth century B.C., obviously," he mumbled, hard at work again on the dials, "but just idle chatter about the rice crop, the barbarians from the south, and such. That is the difficulty; I have to listen to volumes of that sort of thing before I chance on an authentic beginning and record it. But I have been doing just that—and succeeding!" He slapped his hand on a loose pile of scrawled pages that stood upon the desk. "Here are my first successes, fragmentary as yet, but I'm on the way. I have traced a number of important events back to their sources and recorded the very words of their originators at the precise moment of inception. Of course the translations are rough and quite colloquial—but that can be corrected later. My study of beginnings has begun."

I'm afraid I left the professor's company at that time. I did want to hear the ball game and I regret to say that it was the last time that I or anyone else ever saw him alive. The sheets of paper he so valued were taken to be the ravings of an unwell mind, their true worth misunderstood, and they were discarded. I have salvaged some of them and now present them to the public, who can truly judge their real worth. For fragmentary as they are, they still cast the strong light of knowledge into many a darkened corner of history that has been obscured in the past.

". . . even though it is a palace it is still my home, and it is too small by far with my new stepmother, who is a bitz. I had hoped to continue in my philosophy studies, but it is impossible here. Guess I better run the army down to the border; there may be trouble there."

Alexander, Macedonia, 336 B.C.

". . . hot is not Ye word for it, and alle of VIRGINIA is like an Oven this summer. When Opportunity arose to earn a little l.s.d. running a Survey line through the hills I grabbed it before M.F. could change his Minde. That is how I met ——— today (forgot his name, must ask him tomorrow) in the Taverne. We did have an Ale together and did both complain mightily upon the Heat. With one thing leading to Another as they are wont to do, we had more Ales and he did Confide in me. He is a member of a secret club named, I think since Memory is hazy here, The Sons of Liberty, or some such. . . ."

George Washington, 1765

"France has lost its greatness when an honest inventor gains no profit from his onerous toil. I have neglected my practice for months now, perfecting my handy Hacker Supreme Salami Slicer. I should have earned a fortune selling the small models to every butcher in France. But no!, the Convention uses the large model without paying a sou to me, and the butchers are naturally reluctant now to purchase."

J. I. Guillotine, M.D., 1791

"My head doth ache as though I suffereth an ague, and if I ever chance on the slippery-fingered soddish son of an ill-tempered whore who dropped that night-vessel in Fetter Lane, I will roundly thrash him to within an inch of his life, and perhaps a bit beyond. Since arrival in London I have learned the neatness of step and dexterity of motion needed to avoid the contents of the many vessels emptied into the street, but this is the first time there was need to dodge the container itself. Had I moved a trifle quicker this body of crockery in motion would have continued in motion. But my head doth ache. As soon as it is better I must think on this; there is the shade of an idea here."

Sir Isaac Newton, 1682

"I. is afraid that F. knows! If he does I have had it. If I. was not so seductively attractive I would find someone else's bed—but she does lead me on so. She says she can sell some of her jewelry and buy those three ships she was looking at. The last place I want to go is to the damn Spice Islands, right now at the height of the Madrid season. But F. is king, and if he finds out . . .!"

(Attributed to Cristoforo Colombo of Genoa, 1492, but derivation is obscure.)

"Am I glad I got little Pierre the Erector Set. As soon as he is asleep I'll grab the funny tower he just made. I know the Exposition Committee won't use anything like this, but it will keep them quiet for a while."

Alexandre Gustave Eiffel, 1888

"Woe unto China! Crop failures continue this year and the depression is getting worse. Millions unemployed. The only plan that seems at all workable is this construction project that Wah Ping-Ah is so hot about. He says it will give a shot in the arm to the economy and get the cash circulating again. But what a screwball idea! Build a wall fifteen hundred miles long! He wants to use his own initials and call it the WPA project, but I'm going to call it something different and tell the people it's to keep the barbarians out, as you can always sell them on defense appropriations if you scare them enough."

Emperor Shih Hwang-ti, 252 B.C.

"There will be a full moon tonight so I'll have enough light to find that balcony. I hate to take a chance going near that crazy family, but Maria is the hottest piece of baggage in town! She made her kid sister Julie, the buck-toothed wonder!, promise to have the window unlocked."

Romeus Montague, 1562

(Extract from the ship's log.) "Made a landfall today on a hunk of rock. What navigation! We head

for Virginia and end up in Massachusetts! If I ever
catch the Quaker brat who stole the compass . . .!!!"
                              The brig Mayflower, 1620

There are many more like this, but these samples will
suffice to prove that Professor Hakachinik was a genius
far ahead of his time, and a man to whom the students
of history owe an immeasurable debt.

Since there have been many rumors about the professor's death, I wish to go on record now and state the
entire truth. I was the one who discovered the professor's
body, so I know whereof I speak. It is a lie and a canard
that the good man committed suicide; indeed he was in
love with life and was cut off in his prime, and I'm sure
he looked forward to many more productive years. Nor
was he electrocuted, though his TAP machine was close
by and fused and melted as though a singularly large
electrical current had flowed through it. The official records read heart failure and for want of a better word this
description will have to stand, though in all truth the
cause of death was never determined. The professor appeared to be in fine health and in the pink of condition,
though of course he was dead. Since his heart was no
longer beating, heart failure seemed to be a satisfactory
cause of death to enter in the records.

In closing let me state that when I discovered the professor he was seated at his desk, his head cocked toward
the loudspeaker and his pen clutched in his fingers.
Under his hand was a writing pad with an incomplete
entry what he appeared to be writing when death struck.

I make no conclusion about this, but merely record it as a statement of fact.

The writing is in Old Norse, which, for the benefit of those not acquainted with this interesting language, I have translated into modern English:

". . . this meeting will come to order and if you don't put those mead horns away there'll be a few cracked skulls around here, I tell you. Now, order of business. There have been reports of tent caterpillars in Yggdrasill and some dead branches, but we'll get onto that later. Of more pressing interest is the sandy concrete that has been found cracking in foundations of Bifrost Bridge. I want to—just one moment—this is supposed to be a closed meeting and there is someone listening in. Thor, will you please take care of that eavesdropper. . . ."

THE PAD—
A STORY OF
THE DAY AFTER
THE DAY AFTER
TOMORROW

n the expansive, expensive atmosphere of Sardi's
Topside, two hundred stories above the city, a pretty
girl was no novelty, nor a beautiful one either for that
matter. So the redhead in the green suit, who would
certainly have drawn stares, turned heads, on the lower
levels, received no attention here at all until she stopped
at Ron Lowell-Stein's table and slapped him. A good,
roundhouse smack right across the kisser.

His bodyguards, who now made up for their earlier
inattention with an exaggerated display of muscle,
grabbed her and squeezed her, and one even went so far
as to push a gun against the base of her spine.

"Go ahead and have them kill me," she said, shaking
her lovely, shoulder-length hair while an angry flush suf-

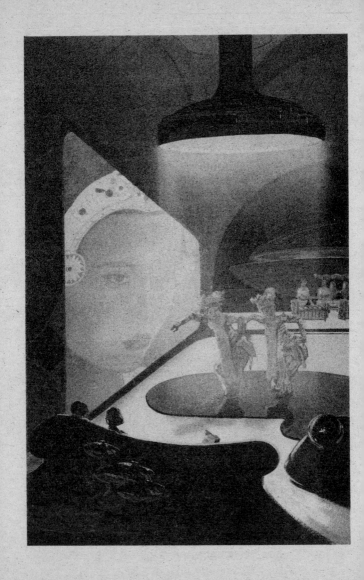

fused the whiteness of her skin. "Add murder to your list of other crimes."

Ron, who rose at once because he was always polite to women, dismissed the bodyguards with a tilt of his head and said, "Would you care to sit down and tell me to which crimes you are referring?"

"Don't play the hypocrite with me, you juvenile Don Juan. I'm talking about my friend, Dolores, the girl whom you ruined."

"Is she ruined? I frankly thought she would be good for many years to come."

This time he caught her wrist before she could connect, proof that the years of polo, copter-hockey, and skeet shooting had toned his muscles and reflexes well. "It seems rather foolish to stand here like this. Can we not sit and fight in undertones like civilized people? I'll order us Black Velvet, that is champagne and stout if you have never tried it, which is a great soother and nerve settler."

"I'll not sit with a man like you," she said as she sat down, firmly pressed into place by the strength of that polo-playing wrist.

"I am Ron Lowell-Stein, the man you hate, but you have not introduced yourself . . .?"

"It's none of your damn business."

"Women should leave swearing to men, who do it so much better." He looked up as one of his bodyguards pulled a printed sheet from his pocketfax and handed it over. "Beatrice Carfax," he read. "I'll call you Bea since I have no liking for these classic names. Father . . . Mother . . . born . . . why you sweet thing, you are only twenty-two. Blood type O; occupation, dancer." His eyes jumped across to her, moved slowly down her torso. "I like that," he said, barely audibly. "Dancers have such beautifully muscled bodies."

She blushed again at the obviousness and pushed away the crystal beaker of dark and bubbling liquid that had been set before her, but he firmly slid it back.

"I do not feel that I have ruined your friend Dolores," he said. "In fact, I thought I was doing her a favor. However, because you are so attractive and forthright I shall give her fifty thousand dollars, a dowry that I know will unruin her in the eyes of any prospective husband."

Beatrice gasped at the sum. "You can't mean this."

"But I do. There is only one condition attached. That you have dinner with me tonight. After which we shall see a performance of the Yugoslavian State Ballet."

"Do you think that you can work your will upon me?" she said hotly.

"Oh, goodness me," he said, touching his pristine handkerchief to the corners of his eyes. "I do not mean to laugh but I have not heard that phrase in, well, I have never heard it spoken aloud, to be exact. I like you, my Bea. You are one of nature's blessings with your sincere naïveté and round little bottom and my chauffeur will pick you up at seven. And, in answer to your question, I shall be frank with you, franker than with most girls who seem to expect some aura of romanticism, yes, I do expect to work my will upon you."

"You cannot!"

"Fine, then you have nothing to fear. Please wear your gold sequin dress; I'm looking forward greatly to seeing you in it."

"What are you talking about? I don't own a gold dress."

"You do now. It will be delivered before you reach home."

Before she could protest the headwaiter appeared and said, *"Scusi mille,* Mr. Lowell-Stein, but your luncheon guests are here."

Two balding and rounded businessmen came up, Brazilians from the look of them. As the men shook hands, the bodyguards helped Bea to her feet and, with subtle pressures, moved her toward the exit. Preserving her dignity with an effort she shrugged away from them and made her own way out of the door. Once on the walkway, in a state of considerable confusion, she automatically took the turnings and changes that brought her home, to the apartment she shared with her ruined friend, Dolores.

"Oh, my sainted mother," Dolores squealed when Beatrice came in, "will you just look at this!" This was a dress that Dolores held out, fresh from its tissue wrappings, a garment of artistic cut and impeccable design that shimmered and reflected the lights with an infinite number of golden mirrors, that in the luxury of its appearance seemed to be spun from real gold. In fact it was pure eighteen-karat gold, though neither girl knew it.

"It's from him," Beatrice said as coldly as she could, turning away, though not without an effort, from the seductive garment. Then she explained what had happened, and when she had finished Dolores stroked the dress and smiled, and spoke.

"Then you're going to date him," she said. "Not for my sake, of course, what's fifty thousand, I mean, you know. Go out for your own sake enjoy, enjoy."

Beatrice gave a little gasp. "Do you mean you wish me to go out with him? After what he did to you?"

"Well, it's done, and maybe we should at least profit from it. I'll go halfies with you on the loot. And you'll get a good meal out of it. But take the advice of one who knows—stay out of that backseat of his car."

"You never told me the details. . . ."

"Don't sound so stuffy. It's not so sordid, not like in the grubby back of some college kid's car. It was after the theater; I was waiting for a cab when this big car pulls up and he offers to drive me home. What's the harm? What with a driver and two mugs in the front seat. But who was to know the windows could turn dark, that the lights would fade, while the whole damn back of the car got turned into a bed with silk sheets, soft music, drinks. To be truthful, honey, it happened so sudden and unreal, like in a dream, I didn't even know that it was happening until it was over and I was getting out of the car. At least you'll get a meal. All I got was a run in my stocking plus I saved the cab fare."

Beatrice thought about this, then looked shocked. "You are not suggesting for a moment that—you know what will happen to me too? I'm not that kind of girl!"

"Neither was I. But I never stood a chance."

"Well I do!" Spoken firmly with her sweet jaw pushed forward stubbornly, the lift of righteous wrath in her gray-green eyes. "No man can force me to . . . do anything against my will."

"You show 'em, honey," Dolores said, caressing the dress. "And enjoy your dinner."

At six a liveried footman brought perfume. Aperge. And in a quart bottle, too.

At six-thirty another uniformed footman brought a mutation smoke-gray mink stole and a note, which read, "To keep your precious shoulders warm."

The golden dress was sleeveless and strapless, and the stole did go with it, and the effect in the mirror was stunning. At seven, when the door annunciator hummed again, she was ready and she stalked out, head high and proud. She would show him.

The footman who escorted her said, "Mr. Lowell-Stein has sent his personal copter instead of his car and has said . . ." He touched a button on his jacket and Ron's melodious voice spoke, saying, "The hastier the transport, the sooner you will be with me, my darling."

"Lead the way," she said sharply—though secretly she was glad not to be traveling in his automotive automated bedroom. Though there was always the possibility that the copter might hold its secrets as well.

If it did, it did not reveal them to her. Instead it carried her swiftly and surely to a marble balcony high on the glossy flank of Lowell-Stein House: that remarkable structure, office building and home, that was the seat of power of the Lowell-Stein World Industries. Its master handed her down himself.

"You are lovely, charming, welcome to my home," he said, tanned, handsome, and respectable, the perfect host. Beatrice decided on the bold course, hoping to gain the emotional upper hand.

"This is a very nice copter," she said, as coldly as she could. "Particularly since it doesn't turn into a flying bagnio at the touch of a button."

"But it does, though that is not for you. For you, dinner and the theater first."

"How dare you!"

"I dare nothing. You dare by coming here; you told me that. Now step inside"—the glass wall rose as they approached then sank behind them—"and have a cocktail. I am old-fashioned so we shall have a traditional drink. A Martini. Vodka or gin—which do you prefer?"

Ron pointed to Goya's *Maja Desnuda,* the original, of course, which whisked from sight disclosing a window behind which moved, in an apparently endless stream, bottle after bottle of every brand of vodka and gin ever manufactured since the world was young. Beatrice concealed her ignorance, quite well she thought, not only of the preferred brand but of the very nature of the Martini itself, by waving gently and saying, "You're the host, why don't you choose for both of us?"

"Capital. We shall have Bombay gin and essence of Noilly Prat, at a ratio of a thousand to one—the way it should be served."

The automated bar heard him and the bottles whizzed by the window and stopped and Queen Victoria frowned down upon them. The glass fell away and a chrome arm plucked out the bottle, opened it, tilted it, poured its contents into the air.

"Oh," Beatrice gasped as the liquid fell toward the rug in a transparent stream.

"A bit showy," he said, "but I like things that are done with style," as, at the last instant, a goblet popped out from a hidden niche and caught the drink, every drop.

It was charming to watch, a functional mobile that entertained with its sprightly motions, concluded by producing the desired drink. The silver band on the goblet was caught by a magnetic field and lifted to eye level, floating freely in the air before them. A chime sounded and an atomizer of vermouth essence sprang out on the end of a cunningly jointed arm and poised itself above the container. Ron reached out a casual finger and touched the bulb, which sent a delicate spray across the surface of the gin.

"I like the personal touch," he said. "I feel that it makes the drink."

Then—one, two, three—a cryogenic tube of liquid helium dipped and spun and lifted away, chilling the drink exactly to within a thousandth of the required degree, and a tray, with two glasses cooled to the same temperature as the liquid, appeared on the end of a telescoping gilded arm to the accompaniment of another chime and Ron asked, "Onion or lemon peel?"

"Whichever you suggest," she laughed, enchanted by the device.

"Both," he smiled. "Let us be sybarites tonight." A tube delivered the onions, forked fingers the slices of lemon, and he handed her her glass.

"A toast," he said, "to our love."

"Don't be rude," she told him, sipping. "I think this is quite good."

"To know it is to love it. I was not rude. I was just reminding you that before the night is gone you will have enjoyed ecstasy."

"Nothing of the sort." She put the drink down, and her foot as well. "I am hungry and I wish to go out and eat."

"Forgive me for not telling you, but we are dining at home. I know you will enjoy the meal, it's ristaffel, your favorite, since I know how wild you are about Indone-

sian food." As he spoke he touched her elbow and led her
toward the dining room. "We shall begin with loempia.
then on to nasi-goreng sambal olek, and for the wine—
the wine!—I have discovered the perfect wine to accompany this exotic meal."

Music swelled as the gamelan orchestra began to play
and the temple dancers glided forth. The table was already set and the first course served and steaming, the
tiers of cups of spices and sauces rotating slowly. Beatrice
knew that the rice would be perfect and fluffy. She did
love this food, but he took too much for granted. She
would be firm, even embarrass him.

"I used to like this," she said, trying to look bored—
while saliva rose unbidden, brought forth by the delightful odors, "but no more. What I prefer is . . ." What? She
tried to think of something exotic. "I really prefer . . .
Danish food, those delightful open sandwiches."

"To think of the terrible mistake I almost made," Ron
said. "Remove this meal."

Beatrice recoiled as the floor opened and the food
dishes, table, chairs, dropped through the yawning gap.
An instant before the floor closed again she heard the
beginning of a terrible crash. Good God, he had thrown
it all away, silverware, crystal, the lot. The orchestra and
dancers were whisked from their podium and for a
dreadful moment she was afraid they were bound for the
incinerator as well.

"Do you like Rembrandt?" he asked, pointing to an
immense painting that covered the rear wall. She turned
to look. " 'The Night Watch,' one of my favorites."

"I thought it was in Holland . . ." she began, then

turned her head at a sound behind her and could not finish.

A long, oaken table with two matching refectory chairs had appeared and was laden with tier upon tier of food.

"Smørrebrød," Ron said, "to be correct, since they are not really sandwiches. There are five hundred here, so I'm sure you will find your favorites. And beer, Tuborg F. F., of course. This is the only fine food that is to be eaten with beer, and akvavit, the sly Danish snaps, served frozen in a block of ice. There are rules, you know."

She had not known, but she was learning. She served herself and ate, and her thoughts flickered like the candles before her. Before she was through eating she was stern and firm again, because she knew full well what was happening.

"You think you can buy me with your money," she told him, as she spooned up the last mouthful of røde grød med fløde. I am supposed to be impressed, grateful for all this, so grateful that I will let you do . . . what you want to do."

"Not at all." He smiled, and his smile was sincerely charming. "I will not deny that there are girls that can be bought with trinkets and meals, but not you. All this, as you so charmingly put it, is here merely for our pleasure while I am determining what your excuse will be."

"I don't understand."

"You will. In simpler cultures lovers clasp to one another in mutual agreement, no aggressor, no loser. We have lost this simplicity and substituted for it a ritualized game. It is called seduction. Women are seduced by men, therefore remain pure. When in reality they have both enjoyed the union of love, mankind's greatest glory and pleasure, and the word seduction is just the excuse the women use to permit it. Every woman has some hidden excuse that she calls seduction, and the artifice of man is in finding that excuse."

"Not I!"

"Yes, you. Yours is not one of the common ones. You will not seek the simple excuse of excessive drink, rough force, simple gratitude, or anything so plebeian. But we shall find it; before dawn we will know."

"I'll hear no more," she said, dropping her spoon and standing. "I wish to leave for the theater now." Once out of this place she knew she would be safe; she would not return.

"By all means, permit me," he held out his arm and she took it. They walked toward the far wall, which lifted silently to reveal a theater within which there were just two seats. "I have hired the entire Yugoslavian company for the evening; they are waiting to begin."

Speechless she sat, and by the end of the performance her mind was still as unsettled as when she had come in. As they applauded she waited, tensely, for him to make his move, so tightly wound that she started visibly when he took her hand.

"You must not," he said, "be afraid of me or of violence. That is not for you, my darling. For you, for us now there is a glass of simple cognac while we discuss the delightful Serbo-Croatian performance that we have just seen."

They exited through the only door, which led now to a brocaded room where a Hungarian violinist played gypsy airs. As they seated themselves at the table a tail-

coated waiter appeared carrying a bottle on a plush cush-
ion. He placed it, with immense care, upon the center of
the table.

"I trust no one but myself to open a bottle like this: the
corks are fragile as dust," Ron said, then added, "I imagine that you have never tasted Napoleon brandy before?"

"If it's from California I have," she told him, with all
sincerity. He closed his eyes.

"No," he said in a slightly choked voice, "it is not from
the State of California, but comes from France, the land
of the mother of wines. Distilled, bottled and laid gently
down during the short but glorious reign of the Emperor
Napoleon Bonaparte. . . ."

"But that must be hundreds and hundreds of years
ago?"

"Precisely. Each year this emperor of cognacs grows a
little, grows more scarce as well. I have men working for
me whose only occupation is to scour the world for more,
to pay any price. I will not profane a conversation about
beauty by mentioning what was paid for this one. You
must judge for yourself if it was worth it."

As he talked he had been working delicately and skill-
fully to remove the cork without damaging it. With a
faint gasping sound it at last slid free and was placed
reverently on a napkin. Into each round-bellied snifter he
then poured but a golden half inch and gave one to her.

"Breathe in the bouquet first, before you take the
smallest sip," he told her, and she obeyed.

A hush fell on the room as they touched the glasses to
their lips and she raised her face in awe, tears in eyes,
saying, "Why . . . it's, it's . . ."

"I know," he said with a whisper, and as he leaned

forward the dim lights darkened even more and the fiddler slipped from sight. His lips brushed the white, bare flesh of her shoulder, kissed it, then moved to her throat.

"Ohh," she gasped, and raised her hand to caress his head. "No!" she said even louder, and pulled away.

"Very close," he smiled, leaning back in his chair. "Very close indeed. You are a creature of ardent passions; we have but to find the key."

"Never," she said finally, and he laughed.

As they finished their brandy the lights grew brighter and, unnoticed, a silvery blade flashed from the leg of her chair, nicked the hem of her skirt, then vanished. Ron took her hand, and when she rose the dress began to unravel and a rain of golden particles fell to the door.

"My dress," she gasped as she clutched at the disintegrating edge. "What's happening to it?"

"It is going," he said, then seated himself again so he could look on in comfort.

Faster and faster the process went and she could not stop it until, within moments, the dress was gone and, like heaped bullion, a golden mound rested about her feet.

"Black lace against white flesh," he said, smiling approval. "You did that just for me. With sweet pink ribbons for your stockings."

"This is crude and rude of you and I hate you. Give me back my clothes," she said fiercely, fists clenched at her sides, too proud to attempt to cover her wispy undergarments with her hands.

"Bravo. You are a redhead of temperament and I have to admire you. Through that door you will find a dressing room and bathing costume, for we shall swim."

"I don't want . . ." she said, but to no avail for the floor moved and carried her through the door into a discreet and elegant boudoir where a black-and-white-garbed French maid was waiting. The maid had an elegantly simple, one-piece white bathing suit on her arm, and she smiled as padded arms gripped Beatrice and flashing devices stripped her remaining clothes from her in an instant.

"Do not fret zee pretty head, mademoiselle," the maid said, holding out the suit. "They were of no value and zee replacements you shall treasure for years, if you please."

"I've been rushed, but I have no choice. None of this will do him any good," Beatrice said, then tried to pull away as sudden clamps seized her again and something small and cold and solid was inserted into each of her delicate nostrils.

"How wonderful is the modern science," the maid said as she patted away the last wrinkle on the skintight suit, which fitted to perfection. "Remember to breathe only through your nose and it will be like fresh breezes. *Au revoir—et bonne chance.*"

Before Beatrice could protest or her raised hand could touch her nose the floor opened and she fell through into the water. She kept her mouth closed and sank under its luminescent surface and found she could breathe as easily as she had always done. The sensation was wonderful, or novel to say the least. There was music, carried to her ears clearly by the conducting water, white sand glinting below. She dived and turned and would have laughed aloud, if she were able, her lovely red hair streaming behind her.

Ron swam up, handsome and tanned in a pair of white

trunks to match her suit, and smiled charmingly—then twisted under and tickled her foot. She turned, smiling too, and darted away, but he followed and they did a breathless dance of three dimensions through the crystal water, around and about, free, unhampered, happy.

Deliciously tired, she floated, suspended, her eyes closed, and felt his arms against her back and the entire strong length of his body against hers and his lips on hers and hers answering. . . .

"No . . ." she said aloud, and a great bubble arose from her mouth. Her fingers tore at her nostrils and there was a sudden, brief pain as the devices were pulled free and fell, twinkling down from her hand. "I would rather die first," she said with the last of her air.

With a gurgling woosh the pool emptied and they sat on the damp sand below. "Woman of will," Ron said, handing her an acre-sized white towel, "I do love you. Now we shall dance, a gavotte; you will enjoy that. There is a string quartet and we will wear the costume of the proper time, you gorgeous in high white wig and low, wide décolletage . . ."

"No. I'm going home." She shivered and wrapped the towel tighter about her body.

"Of course. Dancing would be too commonplace for you. Instead we will . . ."

"No. My clothes. I'm going. You cannot stop me."

He bowed, graceful as always, and gestured her toward a door that had opened in the wall. "Dress yourself; I said violence was not for you. Violence is not your excuse."

"I h-have no excuse," she said through chattering

teeth, and wondered why she shivered since she was so warm.

The little maid was waiting and stripped her down and dried her while a miraculous machine did her hair in seconds, though, in all truth, Beatrice was not aware of this, or even aware of being unaware, as her thoughts darted and spun like maddened butterflies. Only when the maid offered her a dress did she order her thoughts, push it away, push aside the closets of awe-inspiring garments, all her size, to find a simple black suit buried in the back. It had a curve-hugging and breathless simplicity, but it was the best she could do. Powdered, manicured, made up, she had no awareness of it or of the passing of time until, born anew, she stood before him in a chaste and oak-paneled room.

"A last drink," he said, nodding at the Napoleon brandy on the table.

"I'm going," she shouted, because for some reason she wanted to stay. Hurling herself past him she tore open the door on the far wall and slammed it behind her. A stairway stretched up and down and she ran down it, flight after flight, gasping for breath, until she could run no more. For a moment she rested against the wall, then straightened and touched her hair, opened the door and stepped through into the same room she had left high above.

"A last drink," he said, lifting the bottle.

Speechless this time, she ran, closed the door, climbed upwards, higher, until her strength was gone and the stairs ended with a dusty fire door leading to the roof.

Opening it she threw herself through into the same room she had left far below.

"A last drink," he said, decanting the golden drops, then glancing up to notice how her eyes flew to the other doors around the room. "All doors, all halls, all stairs, lead back here," he said, not unkindly. "You must have this drink. Sit. Rest. Drink. A toast. Here's to love, my darling."

Exhausted, she held the glass in both hands, warming it with the heat of her body, then drank. It was heavenly and his face was close beside hers and his lips were whistling in her ear.

"Would you believe," the hushed sibilants sounded, "would you believe that this brandy contains a drug that destroys your will to say no? Resistance is useless, you are mine."

"No, no . . ." her lips said, while her arms said yes, yes, and pulled her to him. No, no, never, never, and darkness descended.

"Drugs, mind-destroying drugs," she said later, in the warm darkness, their fingertips just touching, cool sheets against her back, her voice a little smug and satisfied. "There was no other way, drugs against my will."

"Do you believe," his shocked voice answered, "that I would put anything at all in that brandy? Of course not, my darling. We have just found your excuse, that is all."

I F

W. e are there; we are correct. The computations were perfect. That is our destination below."

"You are a worm," 17 said to her companion, 35, who resembled her every way other than in number. "Yes—that is the correct place. But we are nine years too early. Look at the meter."

"I am a worm. I shall free you of the burden of my useless presence." 35 removed her knife from the scabbard and tested the edge, which proved to be exceedingly sharp. She placed it against the white wattled width of her neck and prepared to cut her throat.

"Not now," 17 hissed. "We are shorthanded already and your corpse would be valueless to this expedition. Get us to the correct time at once. Our power is limited, you may remember."

"It shall be done as you command," 35 said as she slithered to the bank of controls. 44 had ignored the talk, keeping her multicellular eyes focused intently on the power control bank: constantly making adjustments

with her spatulate fingers in response to the manifold dials.

"That is it," 17 announced, rasping her hands together with pleasure. "The correct time, the correct place. We must descend and make our destiny. Give praise to the Saur of All, who rules the destinies of all."

"Praise Saur," her two companions muttered, all of their attention on the controls.

Straight down from the blue sky the globular vehicle fell. It was round and featureless, save for the large rectangular port on the bottom now, and made of some sort of green metal, perhaps anodized aluminum, though it looked harder. It had no visible means of flight or support, yet it fell at a steady and controlled rate. Slower and slower it moved until it dropped from sight behind the ridge at the northern end of Johnson's Lake, just at the edge of the tall pine grove. There were fields nearby, with cows, who did not appear at all disturbed by the visitor. No human being was in sight to view the landing beside the path that cut in from the lake here: a scuffed dirt trail that led to the highway.

An oriole sat on a bush and warbled sweetly; a small rabbit hopped from the field to nibble a stem of grass. This bucolic and peaceful scene was interrupted by the scuff of feet down the trail and a high-pitched and singularly monotonous whistling. The bird flew away, a touch of soundless color, while the rabbit disappeared into the hedge. A boy came over the rise from the direction of the lake shore. He wore ordinary boy clothes and carried a schoolbag in one hand, a homemade cage of wire screen in the other. In the cage was a small lizard which clung to the screen, its eyes rolling in what presumably was fear. The boy, whistling shrilly, trudged along the path and into the shade of the pine grove.

"Boy," a high-pitched and tremulous voice called out. "Can you hear me, boy?"

"I certainly can," the boy said, stopping and looking around for the unseen speaker. "Where are you?"

"I am by your side, but I am invisible. I am your fairy godmother. . . ."

The boy made a rude sound by sticking out his tongue and blowing across it while it vibrated. "I don't believe in invisibility or fairy godmothers. Come out of those woods, whoever you are."

"All boys believe in fairy godmothers," the voice said, but a worried tone edged the words now. "I know all kinds of secrets. I know your name is Don and . . ."

"Everyone knows my name is Don and no one believes anymore in fairies. Boys now believe in rockets, submarines, and atomic energy."

"Would you believe in space travel?"

"I would."

Slightly relieved the voice came on stronger and deeper. "I did not wish to frighten you, but I am really from Mars and have just landed. . . ."

Don made the rude noise again. "Mars has no atmosphere and no observable forms of life. Now come out of there and stop playing games."

After a long silence the voice said, "Would you consider time travel?"

"I could. Are you going to tell me that you are from the future?"

With relief: "Yes I am."

"Then come out where I can see you."

"There are some things that the human eye should not look upon. . . ."

"Horseapples! The human eye is okay for looking at anything you want to name. You come out of there so I can see who you are—or I'm leaving."

"It is not advisable." The voice was exasperated. "I can prove I am a temporal traveler by telling you the answers to tomorrow's mathematics test. Wouldn't that be nice? Number one, 1.76. Number two. . . ."

"I don't like to cheat, and even if I did you can't cheat on the new math. Either you know it or you fail it. I'm—going to count to ten, then I'm leaving."

"No, you cannot! I must ask you a favor. Release that common lizard you have trapped and I will give you three wishes—I mean, answer three questions."

"Why should I let it go?"

"Is that the first of your questions?"

"No. I want to know what's going on before I do anything. This lizard is special. I never saw another one like it around here."

"You are right. It is an Old World acrodont lizard of the order Rhiptoglossa, commonly called a chameleon."

"It is!" Don was really interested now. He squatted in the path and took a red-covered book from his schoolbag and laid it on the ground. He turned the cage until the lizard was on the bottom and placed it carefully on the book. "Will it really turn color?"

"To an observable amount, yes. Now if you release her . . ."

"How do you know it's a her? Is it your time-traveler knowledge-of-the past again?"

"If you must know, yes. The creature was purchased from a pet store by one Jim Benan, and she is one of a pair. They were both released two days ago when Benan, deranged by the voluntary drinking of a liquid containing quantities of ethyl alcohol, sat on the cage. The other, unfortunately, died of his wounds, and this one alone survives. The release . . ."

"I think this whole thing is a joke and I'm going home now. Unless you come out of there so I can see who you are."

"I warn you . . ."

"Goodbye." Don picked up the cage. "Hey, she turned sort of brick red!"

"Do not leave. I will come forth."

Don looked on, with a great deal of interest, while the creature walked out from between the trees. It was blue, had large and goggling, independently moving eyes, wore a neatly cut brown jumpsuit, and had a pack slung on its back. It was also only about seven inches tall.

"You don't much look like a man from the future," Don said. "In fact you don't look like a man at all. You're too small."

"I might say that you are too big: size is a matter of relevancy. And I am from the future, though I am not a man."

"That's for sure. In fact you look a lot like a lizard." In sudden inspiration, Don looked back and forth at the traveler and at the cage. "In fact you look a good deal like this chameleon here. What's the connection?"

"That is not to be revealed. You'll now do as I command or I will injure you gravely." 17 turned and waved toward the woods. "35, this is an order. Appear and destroy that leafed growth over there."

Don looked on with increasing interest as the green basketball of metal drifted into sight from under the trees. A circular disk slipped away on one side and a gleaming nozzle, not unlike the hose nozzle on a toy firetruck, appeared through the opening. It pointed toward a hedge a good thirty feet away. A shrill whining began from the depths of the sphere, rising in pitch until it was almost inaudible. Then, suddenly, a thin line of light spat out towards the shrub, which crackled and instantly burst into flame. Within a second it was a blackened skeleton.

"The device is called a roxidizer, and is deadly," 17 said. "Release the chameleon at once or we will turn it on you."

Don scowled. "All right. Who wants the old lizard anyway." He put the cage on the ground and started to open the cover. Then he stopped and sniffed. Picking up the cage again he started across the grass toward the blackened bush.

"Come back!" 17 screeched. "We will fire if you go another step."

Don ignored the lizardoid, which was now dancing up and down in an agony of frustration, and ran to the bush. He put his hand out and apparently right through the charred stems.

"I thought something was fishy," he said. "All that

burning and everything just upwind of me and I couldn't smell a thing." He turned to look at the time traveler, who was slumped in gloomy silence. "It's just a projected image of some kind, isn't it? Some kind of three-dimensional movie." He stopped in sudden thought, then walked over to the still hovering temporal transporter. When he poked at it with his finger he apparently pushed his hand right into it.

"And this thing isn't here either. Are you?"

"There is no need to experiment. I, and our ship, are present only as what might be called temporal echoes. Matter cannot be moved through time, that is an impossibility, but the concept of matter can be temporally projected. I am sure that this is too technical for you. . . ."

"You're doing great so far. Carry on."

"Our projections are here in a real sense to us, though we can only be an image or a sound wave to any observers in the time we visit. Immense amounts of energy are required and almost the total resources of our civilization are involved in this time transfer."

"Why? And the truth for a change. No more fairy godmother and that kind of malarkey."

"I regret the necessity to use subterfuge, but the secret is too important to reveal casually without attempting other means of persuasion."

"Now we get to the real story." Don sat down and crossed his legs comfortably. "Give."

"We need your aid, or our very society is threatened. Very recently, on our time scale, strange disturbances

were detected by our instruments. Ours is a simple
saurian existence, some million or so years in the future,
and our race is dominant. Your race has long since vanished—in a manner too horrible to mention to your
young ears. Now something is threatening our entire
race. Research quickly uncovered the fact that we are
about to be overwhelmed by a probability wave that will
completely destroy us. A great wave of negation is sweep-
ing toward us from our remote past."

"You wouldn't mind tipping me off to what a probability wave is, would you?"

"I will take an example from your own literature. If
your grandfather had died without marrying, you would
not have been born and would not now exist."

"But I do.

"The matter is debatable in the greater xan-probability
universe, but we shall not discuss that now. Our power is
limited. To put the affair simply, we traced our ancestral
lines back through all the various mutations and changes
until we found the individual protolizard from which our
line sprung."

"Let me guess." Don pointed at the cage. "This is the
one?"

"She is." 17 spoke in solemn tones, as befitted the
moment. "Just as somewhen, somewhere there is a proto-
tarsier from which your race sprung, so is there before us
this temporal mother of ours. She will bear young soon,
and they will breed and grow in this pleasant valley. The
rocks near the lake have an appreciable amount of radio-
activity, which will cause mutations. The centuries will

roll by and, one day, our race will reach its heights of glory."

"Sounds great."

"It is—or it will be. But none of this will happen if you do not open that cage."

Don rested his chin on his fist and thought. "You're not putting me on anymore? This is the truth?"

17 drew herself up and waved both arms—or rather her front legs—over her head. "By the Saur of All, I promise," she intoned. "By the stars eternal, the seasons vernal, the clouds, the sky, the matriarchal I . . ."

"Just cross your heart and hope to die, that will be good enough for me."

The lizardoid moved its eyes in concentric circles and performed this ritual.

"Okay then, I'm as softhearted as the next guy when it comes to wiping out whole races."

Don unbent the piece of wire that sealed the cage and opened the top. The chameleon rolled one eye up at him and looked at the opening with the other. 17 watched in awed silence and the time vehicle bobbed closer.

"Get going," Don said, and shook the lizard out into the grass.

This time the chameleon took the hint and scuttled away among the bushes, vanishing from sight.

"That takes care of the future," Don said. "Or the past from your point of view."

17 and the time machine vanished silently and Don was alone again on the path.

"Well you could of at least said thanks before taking off like that. People have more manners than lizards any day I'll tell you that."

He picked up the now-empty cage and his schoolbag and started for home.

He had not heard the quick rustle in the bushes, nor did he see the prowling tomcat with the limp chameleon in its jaws.

MUTE MILTON

With ponderous smoothness the big Greyhound bus braked to a stop at the platform and the door swung open.

"Springville," the driver called out. "Last stop!" The passengers stirred in the aisle and climbed down the steps into the glare of the sun. Sam Morrison sat patiently, alone, on the wide rear seat, waiting until the last passengers were at the door before he put the cigar box under his arm, rose, and followed them. The glare of sunlight blinded him after the tinted-glass dimness of the bus, and the moist air held the breathless heat of Mississippi summer. Sam went carefully down the steps one-at-a-time, watching his feet, and wasn't aware of the man waiting there until something hard pushed at his stomach.

"What business yuh got in Springville, boy?"

Sam blinked through his steel-rimmed glasses at the big man in the gray uniform who stood before him, prodding him with a short, thick nightstick. He was fat as well as big, and the smooth melon of his stomach bulged out over his belt, worn low about his hips.

"Just passing through, sir," Sam Morrison said and took his hat off with his free hand, disclosing his cut-short grizzled hair. He let his glance slide across the flushed reddened face and the gold badge on the shirt before him, then lowered his eyes.

"An just where yuh goin' to, boy? Don't keep no secrets from me . . ." the voice rasped again.

"Carteret, sir, my bus leaves in an hour."

The only answer was an uncommunicative grunt. The lead-weighted stick tapped on the cigar box under Sam's arm. "What yuh got in there—a gun?"

"No, sir, I wouldn't carry a gun." Sam opened the cigar box and held it out: it contained a lump of metal, a number of small electronic components and a two-inch speaker, all neatly wired and soldered together. "It's a . . . a radio, sir."

"Turn it on."

Sam threw a switch and made one or two careful adjustments. The little speaker rattled and there was the squeak of tinny music barely audible above the rumble of bus motors. The red-faced man laughed.

"Now that's what Ah call a real nigger radio . . . piece uh trash." His voice hardened again. "See that you're on that bus, hear?"

"Yes, sir," Sam said to the receding, sweat-stained back of the shirt, then carefully closed the box. He started toward the colored waiting room but when he passed the window and looked in he saw that it was empty. And there were no dark faces visible anywhere on the street. Without changing pace Sam passed the waiting room and threaded his way between the buses in the cinder parking lot and out of the rear gate. He had lived all of his sixty-seven years in the State of Mississippi so he knew at once that there was trouble in the air—and the only thing to do about trouble was to stay away from it. The streets became narrower and dirtier and he trod their familiar sidewalks until he saw a field-worker in patched overalls turn in to a doorway ahead under the weathered BAR sign. Sam went in after him; he would wait here until a few minutes before the bus was due.

"Bottle of Jax, please." He spread his coins on the damp, scratched bar and picked up the cold bottle. There was no glass. The bartender said nothing. After ringing up the sale he retired to a chair at the far end of the bar with his head next to the murmuring radio and remained there, dark and impenetrable. The only light came from the street outside, and the high-backed booths in the rear looked cool and inviting. There were only a few other customers here, each of them sitting separately with a bottle of beer on the table before him. Sam threaded his way through the close-spaced tables and had already started to slide into the booth near the rear door when he noticed that someone was already there, seated on the other side of the table.

"I'm sorry, I didn't see you," he said and started to get up, but the man waved him back onto the bench and took an airline bag with "TWA" on it from the table and put it down beside him.

"Plenty of room for both," he said and raised his bottle of beer. "Here's looking at you." Sam took a sip from his own bottle, but the other man kept drinking until he had drained half of his before he lowered it with a relaxed sigh. "That's what I call foul beer," he said.

"You seem to be enjoying it," Sam told him, but his slight smile took the edge from his words.

"Just because it's cold and wet—but I'd trade a case of it for a bottle of Bud or a Ballantine."

"Then you're from the North, I imagine?" Sam had thought so from the way he talked, sharp and clipped. Now that his eyes were getting used to the dimness he could see that the other was a young man in his twenties with medium-dark skin, wearing a white shirt with rolled-up sleeves. His face was taut and the frown wrinkles on his forehead seemed etched there.

"You are damned right, I'm from the North and I'm going back . . ." He broke off suddenly and took another swig of beer. When he spoke again his voice was cautious. "Are you from these parts?"

"I was born not far from here, but right now I live in Carteret, just stopping off here between buses."

"Carteret—that's where the college is, isn't it?"

"That is correct. I teach there."

The younger man smiled for the first time. "That sort of puts us in the same boat. I go to NYU, majoring in economics." He put his hand out. "Charles Wright—everyone but my mother calls me Charlie."

"Very pleased to meet you," Sam said in his slow old-fashioned way. "I am Sam Morrison, and it is Sam on my birth certificate too."

"I'm interested in your college. I meant to stop in there but . . ." Charles broke off suddenly at the sound of a car's engine in the street outside and leaned forward so that he could see out the front door, remaining there until the car ground into gear and moved away. When Charles

dropped back onto the seat Sam could see that there were
fine beads of sweat in the lines of his forehead. He took
a quick drink from his bottle.

"When you were at the bus station you didn't happen
to see a big cop with a big gut, red face all the time?"

"Yes, I met him, he talked to me when I got off the
bus."

"The bastard!"

"Don't get worked up, Charles; he is just a policeman
doing his job."

"Just a . . . !" The young man spat a short, filthy word.
"That's Brinkley, you must have heard of him, toughest
man south of Bombingham. He's going to be elected
sheriff next fall and he's already a Grand Knight of the
Klan, a real pillar of the community."

"Talking like that's not going to do you any good,"
Sam said mildly.

"That's what Uncle Tom said—and as I remember he
was still a slave when he died. Someone has got to speak
up, you can't remain quiet forever."

"You talk like one of those Freedom Riders." Sam
tried to look stern, but he had never been very good at it.

"Well, I am one, if you want to know the truth of it,
but the ride ends right here. I'm going home. I'm scared
and I'm not afraid to admit it. You people live in a jungle
down here; I never realized how bad it could be until I
came down. I've been working on the voter's committee
and Brinkley got word of it and swore he was going to
kill me or put me in jail for life. And you know what? I
believe it. I'm leaving today, just waiting for the car to
pick me up. I'm going back North where I belong."

"I understand that you have your problems up there, too. . . ."

"Problems!" Charlie finished his beer and stood up. "I wouldn't even call them problems after what I've seen down here. It's no paradise in New York—but you stand a chance of living a bit longer. Where I grew up in South Jamaica we had it rough, but we had our own house in a good neighborhood and—you take another beer?"

"No, one is enough for me, thank you."

Charlie came back with a fresh beer and picked up where he had left off. "Maybe we're second-class citizens in the North but at least we're citizens of some kind and can get some measure of happiness and fulfillment. Down here a man is a beast of burden and that's all he is ever going to be—if he has the wrong color skin."

"I wouldn't say that, things get better all the time. My father was a field hand, a son of a slave—and I'm a college teacher. That's progress of a sort."

"What sort?" Charlie pounded the table, yet kept his voice in an angry whisper. "So one-hundredth of one percent of the Negroes get a little education and pass it on at some backwater college. Look, I'm not running you down; I know you do your best. But for every man like you there must be a thousand who are born and live and die in filthy poverty, year after year, without hope. Millions of people. Is that progress? And even yourself— are you sure you wouldn't be doing better if you were teaching in a decent university?"

"Not me," Sam laughed. "I'm just an ordinary teacher and I have enough trouble getting geometry and algebra across to my students without trying to explain topology or Boolean algebra or anything like that."

"What on earth is that Bool . . . thing? I never heard of it."

"It's, well, an uninterpreted logical calculus, a special discipline. I warned you, I'm not very good at explaining these things though I can work them out well enough on paper. That is my hobby, really, what some people call higher mathematics; and I know that if I were working at a big school I would have no time to devote to it."

"How do you know? Maybe they would have one of those big computers—wouldn't that help you?"

"Perhaps, of course, but I've worked out ways of getting around the need for one. It takes a little more time, that's all."

"And how much time do you have left?" Charlie asked quietly, then was instantly sorry he had said it when he saw the older man lower his head without answering. "I take that back, I've got a big mouth, I'm sorry. But I get so angry. How do you know what you might have done if you had had the training, the facilities. . . ." He shut up, realizing that he was getting in deeper every second.

There was only the murmur of distant traffic in the hot, dark silence, the faint sound of music from the radio behind the bar. The bartender stood, switched the radio off, and opened the trap behind the bar to bring in another case of beer. From nearby the sound of the music continued like a remembered echo. Charlie realized that it was coming from the cigar box on the table before them.

"Do you have a radio in that?" he asked, happy to change the subject.

"Yes—well really no, though there is an RF stage."

"If you think you're making sense—you're not. I told you, I'm majoring in economics."

Sam smiled and opened the box, pointing to the precisely wired circuits inside. "My nephew made this, he has a little 'I fix it' shop, but he learned a lot about electronics in the air force. I brought him the equations and we worked out the circuit together."

Charlie thought about a man with electronic training who was forced to run a handyman's shop, but he had the sense not to mention it. "Just what is it supposed to do?"

"It's not really supposed to do anything. I just built it to see if my equations would work out in practice. I suppose you don't know much about Einstein's unified field theory . . . ?" Charlie smiled ruefully and raised his hands in surrender. "It's difficult to talk about. Putting it the simplest way, there is supposed to be a relation between all phenomena, all forms of energy and matter. You are acquainted with the simpler interchanges, heat energy to mechanical energy as in an engine, electrical energy to light . . ."

"The light bulb!"

"Correct. To go further, the postulation has been made that time is related to light energy, as is gravity to light, which has been proved, and gravity to electrical energy. That is the field I have been exploring. I have made certain suppositions that there is an interchange of energy within a gravitic field, a measurable interchange, such as the lines of force that are revealed about a magnetic field by iron particles—no, that's not a good simile—perhaps the ability of a wire to carry a current endlessly under the chilled condition of superconductivity."

"Professor, you have lost me, I'm not ashamed to admit it. Could you maybe give me an example—like what is happening in this little radio here?"

Sam made a careful adjustment and the music gained the tiniest amount of volume. "It's not the radio part that is interesting, that stage really just demonstrates that I have detected the leakage—no, we should call it the differential—between the Earth's gravitic field and that of the lump of lead there in the corner of the box."

"Where is the battery?"

Sam smiled proudly. "That is the point—there is no battery. The input current is derived . . ."

"Do you mean you are running the radio off gravity? Getting electricity for nothing?"

"Yes . . . really, I should say no. It is not quite like that . . ."

"It sure looks like that!" Charlie was excited now, crouching half across the table so he could look into the cigar box. "I may not know anything about electronics but in economics we learn a lot about power sources. Couldn't this gadget of yours be developed to generate electricity at little or no cost?"

"No, not at once, this is just a first attempt . . ."

"But it could eventually and that means—"

Sam thought that the young man had suddenly become sick. His face, just inches away, became shades lighter as the blood drained from it, his eyes were staring in horror as he slowly dropped back and down into his seat. Before Sam could ask him what was the matter a grating voice bellowed through the room.

"Anyone here seen a boy by name of Charlie Wright? C'mon now, speak up, ain't no one gonna get hurt for tellin' me the truth."

"Holy Jesus . . ." Charlie whispered, sinking deeper in the seat. Brinkley stamped into the bar, hand resting on his gun butt, squinting around in the darkness. No one answered him.

"Anybody try to hide him gonna be in trouble!" he shouted angrily. "I'm gonna find that black granny dodger!"

He started toward the rear of the room and Charlie, with his airline bag in one hand, vaulted the back of the booth and crashed against the rear door.

"Come back here, you son of a bitch!"

The table rocked when Charlie's flying heel caught it and the cigar box slid off to the floor. Heavy boots thundered and the door squealed open and Charlie pushed out through it. Sam bent over to retrieve the box.

"I'll kill yuh, so help me!"

The circuit hadn't been damaged; Sam sighed in relief and stood, the tinny music between his fingers.

He may have heard the first shot but he could not have heard the second because the .38 slug caught him in the back of the head and killed him instantly. He crumpled to the floor.

Patrolman Marger ran in from the patrol car outside, his gun ready, and saw Brinkley come back into the room through the door in the rear.

"He got away, damn it, got clear away."

"What happened here?" Marger asked, slipping his gun back into the holster and looking down at the slight, crumpled body at his feet.

"I dunno. He must have jumped up in the way when I let fly at the other one what was running away. Must be another one of them commonists anyway, he was sittin' at the same table."

"There's gonna be trouble about this. . . ."

"Why trouble?" Brinkley asked indignantly. "It's just anutha ol' dead nigger. . . ."

One of his boots was on the cigar box and it crumpled and fractured when he turned away.

SIMULATED TRAINER

Mars was a dusty, frigid hell. Bone dry and blood red. They trudged single file through the ankle-deep sand; in a monotonous duet cursed the nameless engineer who had designed the faulty reconditioners in their pressure suits. The bug hadn't shown during testing of the new suits. It appeared only after they had been using them steadily for a few weeks. The water-absorbers became overloaded and broke down. The Martian atmosphere stood at a frigid sixty degrees centigrade. Inside the suits, they tried to blink the unevaporated sweat from their eyes and slowly cooked in the high humidity.

Morley shook his head viciously to dislodge an itching droplet from his nose. At the same moment, something rust-colored and furry darted across his path. It was the first Martian life they had seen. Instead of scientific curiosity, he felt only anger. A sudden kick sent the animal flying high into the air.

The suddenness of the movement threw him off balance. He fell sideways slowly, dragging his rubberized suit along an upright rock fragment of sharp obsidian.

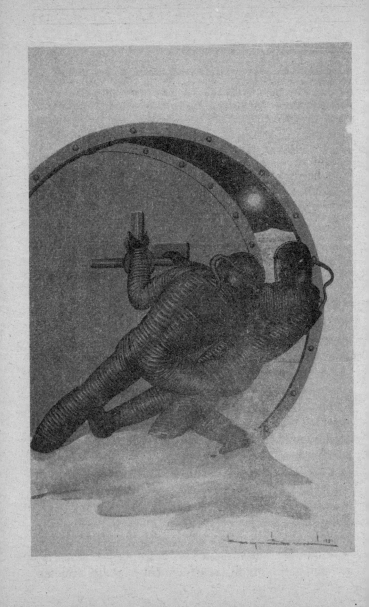

Tony Bannerman heard the other man's hoarse shout in his earphones and whirled. Morley was down, thrashing on the sand with both hands pressed against the ragged tear in the suit leg. Moisture-laden air was pouring out in a steaming jet that turned instantly to scintillating ice crystals. Tony jumped over to him, trying to seal the tear with his own ineffectual gloves. Their faceplates close, he could see the look of terror on Morley's face—as well as the blue tinge of cyanosis.

"Help me—help me!"

The words were shouted so loud they rasped the tiny helmet earphones. But there was no help. They had taken no emergency patches with them. All the patches were in the ship at least a quarter of a mile away. Before he could get there and back, Morley would be dead.

Tony straightened up slowly and sighed. Just the two of them in the ship, there was no one else on Mars who could help. Morley saw the look in Tony's eyes and stopped struggling.

"No hope at all, Tony—I'm dead."

"Just as soon as all the oxygen is gone; thirty seconds at the most. There's nothing I can do."

Morley grated the shortest, vilest word he knew and pressed the red EMERGENCY button set into his glove above the wrist. The ground opened up next to him in the same instant, sand sifting down around the edges of the gap. Tony stepped back as two men in white pressure suits came up out of the hole. They had red crosses on the fronts of their helmets and carried a stretcher. They rolled Morley onto it and were gone back into the opening in an instant.

Tony stood looking sourly at the hole for about a

minute waiting until Morley's suit was pushed back through the opening. Then the sand-covered trapdoor closed and the desert was unbroken once more.

The dummy in the suit weighed as much as Morley and its plastic features even resembled him a bit. Some wag had painted black X's on the eyes. Very funny, Tony thought, he struggled to get the clumsy thing onto his back. On the way back the now-quiet Martian animal was lying in his path. He kicked it aside and it rained a fine shower of springs and gears.

The too-small sun was touching the peaks of the saw-tooth red mountains when he reached the ship. Too late for burial today, it would have to wait until morning. Leaving the thing in the airlock, he stamped into the cabin and peeled off his dripping pressure suit.

It was dark by that time and the things they had called the night-owls began clicking and scratching against the hull of the ship. They had never managed to catch sight of night-owls; that made the sound doubly annoying. He clattered the pans noisily to drown the sound of them out while he prepared the hot evening rations. When the meal was finished and the dishes cleared away, he began to feel the loneliness for the first time. Even the chew of tobacco didn't help; tonight it only reminded him of the humidor of green Havana cigars waiting for him back on Earth.

His single kick upset the slim leg of the mess table, sending metal dishes, pans and silverware flying in every direction.

They made a satisfactory noise and he exacted even greater pleasure by leaving the mess just that way and going to bed.

They had been so close this time, if only Morley had

kept his eyes open! He forced the thought out of his mind and went to sleep.

In the morning he buried Morley. Then, grimly and carefully, he passed the remaining two days until blast off time. Most of the geological samples were sealed away, while the air sampling and radiation recording meters were fully automatic.

On the final day, he removed the recording tapes from the instruments, then carried the instruments themselves away from the ship where they couldn't be caught in the takeoff blast. Next to the instruments he piled all the extra supplies, machinery and unneeded equipment. Shuffling through the rusty sand for the last time, he gave Morley's grave an ironical salute as he passed. There was nothing to do in the ship and not as much as a pamphlet left to read. Tony passed the two remaining hours on his bunk counting the rivets in the ceiling.

A sharp click from the control clock broke the silence and behind the thick partition he could hear the engines begin the warm-up cycle. At the same time, the padded arms slipped across his bunk, pinning him down securely. He watched the panel slip back in the wall next to him and the hypo arm slide through, moving erratically like a snake as its metal fingers sought him out. They touched his ankle and the serpent's tooth of the needle snapped free. The last thing he saw was the needle slipping into his vein, then the drug blacked him out.

As soon as he was under, a hatch opened in the rear bulkhead and two orderlies brought in a stretcher. They wore no suits or masks and the blue sky of Earth was visible behind them.

* * *

Coming to was the same as it always had been. The gentle
glow from the stimulants that brought him up out of it,
the first sight of the white ceiling of the operating room
on Earth.

Only this time the ceiling wasn't visible, it was obscured by the red face and thundercloud brow of Colonel
Stegham. Tony tried to remember if you saluted while in
bed, then decided that the best thing to do was lie quietly.

"Damn it, Bannerman," the colonel growled. "Welcome back on Earth. And why the hell did you bother
coming back? With Morley dead the expedition has to be
counted a failure—and that means not one completely
successful expedition to date."

"The team in number two, sir, how did they do . . . ?"
Tony tried to sound cheerful.

"Terrible. If anything, worse than your team. Both
dead on the second day after landing. A meteor puncture
in their oxygen tank and they were too busy discovering
a new flora to bother looking at any readouts.

"Anyway, that's not why I'm here. Get on some
clothes and come into my office."

He slammed out and Tony scrambled off the bed,
ignoring the touch of dizziness from the drugs. When
colonels speak lieutenants hurry to obey.

Colonel Stegham was scowling out of his window
when Tony came in. He returned the salute and proved
that he had a shard of humanity left in his military soul
by offering Tony one of his cigars. Only when they had
both lit up did he wave Tony's attention to the field
outside the window.

"Do you see that? Know what it is?"

"Yes, sir, the Mars rocket."

"It's going to be the Mars rocket. Right now, it's only a half-completed hull. The motors and instruments are being assembled in plants all over the country. Working on a crash basis the earliest estimate of completion is six months from now.

"The ship will be ready—only we aren't going to have any men to go in her. At the present rate of washout there won't be a single man qualified. Yourself included."

Tony shifted uncomfortably under his gaze as the colonel continued.

"This training program has always been my baby. Dreamed it up and kept bugging the Pentagon until it was finally adapted. We knew we could build a ship that would get to Mars and back, operated by fully automated controls that would fly her under any degree of gravity or free fall. But we needed men who could walk out on the surface of the planet and explore it—or the whole thing would be so much wasted effort.

"The ship and the robot pilot could be tested under simulated flight condition, and the bugs worked out. It was my suggestion, which was adopted, that the men who are to go in the ship should be shaken down in the same way. Two pressure chambers were built, simulated trainers that duplicated Mars in every detail we could imagine. We have been running two-man teams through these chambers for eighteen months now, trying to train them to man the real ship out there.

"I'm not going to tell you how many men we started with, or how many have been casualties because of the necessary realism of the chambers. I'll tell you this much though—we haven't had one successful simulated expedition in all that time. And every man who has broken down or 'died,' like your partner Morley, has been eliminated.

"There are only four possible men left, yourself included. If we don't get one successful two-man team out of you four, the entire program is a washout."

Tony sat frozen, the dead cigar between his fingers. He knew that the pressure had been on for some months now, that Colonel Stegham had been growling around like a gut-shot bear. The colonel's voice cut through his thoughts.

"Psych division has been after me for what they think is a basic weakness of the program. Their feeling is that because it is a training program the men always have it in the back of their minds that it's not for real. They can always be pulled out of a tight hole. Like Morley was, at the last moment. After the results we have had I am beginning to agree with Psych.

"There are four men left and I am going to run one more exercise for each two-man group. This final exercise will be a full dress rehearsal—this time we're playing for keeps."

"I don't understand, Colonel. . . ."

"It's simple." Stegham accented his words with a bang of his fist on the desk. "We're not going to help or pull anyone out no matter how much they need it. This is battle training with live ammunition. We're going to throw everything at you that we can think of—and you are going to have to take it. If you tear your suit this time, why you are going to die in the Martian vacuum just a few feet from all the air in the world."

His voice softened just a bit when he dismissed Tony. "I wish there was some other way to do it, but we have no choice now. We have to get a crew for that ship next month and this is the only way to be sure."

Tony had a three-day pass. He was drunk the first day, hungover sick the second—and boiling mad on the third. Every man on the project was a volunteer so adding deadly realism was carrying the thing too far. He could get out any time he wanted, though he knew what he would look like then. There was only one thing to do: go along with the whole stupid idea. He would do what they wanted and go through with it. And when he had finished the exercise, he looked forward to hitting the colonel right on the end of his big bulbous nose.

He joined his new partner, Hal Mendoza, when he went for his medical. They had met casually at the training lecture before the simulated training began. They shook hands reservedly now, each eying the other with a view to future possibilities. It took two men to make a team and either one could be the cause of death for the other.

Mendoza was almost the physical opposite of Tony, tall and wiry, while Tony was as squat and solid as a tank. Tony's relaxed, almost casual manner was matched by the other man's seemingly tense nerves. Hal chewed nicotine continuously and would obviously have preferred to go back to chain-smoking. His eyes were never still.

Tony forgot his momentary worry with an effort. Hal would have to be good to get this far in the program. He would probably calm down once the exercise was under way.

The medic took Tony next and began the detailed examination.

"What's this?" the medical officer asked Tony as he probed with a swab at his cheek.

"Ouch," Tony said. "Razor cut, my hand slipped while I was shaving."

The doctor scowled and painted on antiseptic, then slapped on a square of gauze.

"Watch all skin openings," he warned. "They make ideal entry routes for bacteria. Never know what you might find on Mars."

Tony started to protest, then let it die in his throat. What was the use of explaining that the real trip—if and when it ever came off—would take 260 days. Any cuts would be well healed in that time, even in frozen sleep.

As always after the medical, they climbed into their flight suits and walked over to the testing building. On the way Tony stopped at the barracks and dug out his chess set and well-thumbed deck of cards. The access door was open in the thick wall of Building Two and they stepped through into the dummy Mars ship. After the medics had strapped them to the bunks the simulated frozen-sleep shots put them under.

Coming to was accompanied by the usual nausea and weakness. No realism spared. On a sudden impulse Tony staggered to the latrine mirror and blinked at his red-eyed, smooth-shaven reflection. He tore the bandage off his cheek and his fingers touched the open cut with the still congealed drop of blood at the bottom. A relaxed sigh slipped out. He had the recurrent bad dream that some day one of these training trips would really be a flight to Mars. Logic told him that the bureaucrats would never forgo the pleasure and publicity of a big send-off. Yet the doubt, like all illogical ones, persisted. At the beginning of each training flight, he had to abolish it again.

The nausea came back with a swoop and he forced it down. This was one exercise where he couldn't waste time. The ship had to be checked. Hal was sitting up on his bunk waving a limp hand. Tony waved back.

At that moment, the emergency communication speaker crackled into life. At first, there was just the rustle of activity in the control office, then the training officer's voice cut through the background noise.

"Lieutenant Bannerman—you awake yet?"

Tony fumbled the mike out of its clip and reported. "Here, sir."

Then the endless seconds of waiting as the radio signal crossed the depths of space to Earth, was received and answered.

"Just a second, Tony," the officer said. He mumbled to someone at one side of the mike, then came back on. "There's been some trouble with one of the bleeder valves in the chamber; the pressure is above Mars norm. Hold the exercise until we pump her back down."

"Yes, sir," Tony said, then killed the mike so he and Hal could groan about the so-called efficiency of the training squad. It was only a few minutes before the speaker came back to life.

"Okay, pressure on the button. Carry on as before."

Tony made an obscene gesture at the unseen man behind the voice and walked over to the single port. He cranked at the handle that moved the crash shield out of the way.

"Well, at least it's a quiet Mars for a change," he said after the ruddy light had streamed in. Hal came up and looked over his shoulder.

"Praise Stegham for that," he said. "The last one, where I lost my partner, was wind all the time. From the shape of those dunes it looks like the atmosphere never moves at all." They stared glumly at the familiar red landscape and dark sky for a long moment, then Tony turned to the controls while Hal cracked out the atmosphere suits.

"Over here—quickly!"

Hal didn't have to be called twice, he was at the board in a single jump. He followed Tony's pointing finger.

"The water meter—it shows the tank's only about half-full!"

They struggled to take off the plate that gave access to the tank compartment. When they laid it aside a small trickle of rusty water ran across the deck at their feet. Tony crawled in with a flashlight and moved it up and down the tubular tanks. His muffled voice echoed inside the small compartment.

"Damn Stegham and his tricks—another 'shock of landing failure.' Connecting pipe split and the water that leaked out has soaked down into the insulating layer; we'll never get it out without tearing the ship apart. Hand me the gunk. I'll plug the leak until we can repair it."

"It's going to be an awfully dry month," Hal said grimly while he checked the rest of the control board.

The first few days were like every other trip. They planted the flag and unloaded the equipment. The observing and recording instruments were set up by the third day; they unshipped the automatic theodolite and started it making maps. By the fourth day they were ready to begin their sample collection.

It was just at this point that they really became aware of the dust.

Tony chewed an unusually gritty mouthful of rations cursing under his breath because there was only a mouthful of water to wash it down with. He swallowed it painfully then looked around the control chamber.

"Have you noticed how dusty it is?" he asked.

"How could you not notice it? I have so much of it inside my clothes I feel like I'm living on an anthill."

Hal stopped scratching just long enough to take a bite of food.

They both looked around and it hit them for the first time just how much dust was in the ship. A red coating on everything, in their food and in their hair. The constant scratch of grit underfoot.

"It must be carried in on our suits," Tony said. "We'll have to clean them off better before coming inside."

It was a good idea—the only trouble was that it did not work. The red dust was as fine as talcum powder and no amount of beating could dislodge it; it just drifted around in a fine haze. They tried to forget the dust, just treating it as one more nuisance Stegham's technicians had dreamed up. This worked for a while, until the eighth day when they couldn't close the outer door of the air lock. They had just returned from a sample-collecting trip. The air lock barely held the two of them plus the bags of rock samples. Taking turns, they beat the dust off each other as well as they could, then Hal threw the cycling switch. The outer door started to close, then stopped. They could feel the increased hum of the door

motor through their shoes, then it cut out and the red
trouble light flashed on.

"Dust!" Tony said. "That damned red dust is in the
works."

The inspection plate came off easily and they saw the
exposed gear train. The red dust had merged into a de-
structive mud with the grease. Finding the trouble was
easier than repairing it, since they had only a few basic
tools in their suit pouches. The big toolbox and all the
solvent that would have made fast work of the job were
inside the ship. But they couldn't be reached until the
door was fixed. And the door couldn't be fixed without
tools. It was a paradoxical situation that seemed very
unfunny.

They worked against time, trying not to look at the
oxygen gauges. It took them almost two hours to clean
the gears as best they could and force the door shut.
When the inner port finally opened, both their oxygen
tanks read EMPTY, and they were operating on the emergency reserves.

As soon as Hal opened his helmet, he dropped on his
bunk. Tony thought he was unconscious until he saw
that the other man's eyes were open and staring at the
ceiling. He cracked open the single flask of medicinal
brandy and forced Hal to take some. Then he had a
double swallow himself and tried to ignore the fact that
his partner's hands were trembling violently. He busied
himself making a better repair of the door mechanism.
By the time he had finished, Hal was off the bunk and
starting to prepare their evening meal.

Outside of the dust, it appeared to be a routine exercise. At first. Surveying and sampling most of the day,

then a few leisure hours before retiring. Hal was a good partner and the best chess player Tony had teamed with to date. Tony soon found out that what he thought was nervousness was nervous energy. Hal was only happy when he was doing something. He threw himself into the day's work and had enough enthusiasm and energy left over to smash the yawning Tony over the chessboard. The two men were quite opposite types and made good teammates.

Everything looked good—except for the dust. It was everywhere, and bit by bit getting into everything. It annoyed Tony, but he stolidly did not let it bother him deeply. Hal was the one that suffered most. It scratched and itched him, setting his temper on edge. He began to have trouble sleeping. And the creeping dust was slowly working its way into every single item of equipment. The machinery was starting to wear as fast as their nerves. The constant presence of the itching dust, together with the acute water shortage was maddening. They were always thirsty and there was nothing they could do about it. They had only the minimum amount of water to last until blast off. Even with drastic rationing, it would barely be enough.

They quarreled over the ration on the thirteenth day and almost came to blows. For two days after that they didn't talk. Tony noticed that Hal always kept one of the sampling hammers in his pocket; in turn, he took to carrying one of the dinner knives.

Something had to crack. It turned out to be Hal.

It must have been the lack of sleep that finally got to him. He had always been a light sleeper, now the tension and the dust were too much. Tony could hear him scratching and turning each night when he forced himself to sleep. He wasn't sleeping too well himself, but at least he managed to get a bit. From the black hollows under Hal's bloodshot eyes it didn't look like Hal was getting any.

On the eighteenth day he cracked. They were just getting into their suits when he started shaking. Not just his hands, but all over. He just stood there shaking until Tony got him to the bunk and gave him the rest of the brandy. When the attack was over he refused to go outside.

"I won't . . . I can't!" He screamed the words. "The suits won't last much longer, they'll fail while we're out there. . . . Hell with the suits—I won't last any longer. . . . We have to go back. . . ."

Tony tried to reason with him. "We can't do that, you know this is a full-scale exercise. We can't get out until the twenty-eight days are up. That's only ten more days, you can hold out until then. That's the minimum figure the army decided on for a stay on Mars—it's built into all the plans and machinery. Be glad we don't have to wait an entire Martian year until the planets get back into conjunction. With deep sleep and atomic drive that's one trouble that won't be faced."

"Shut your goddamned mouth and stop trying to kid me along," Hal shouted. "I don't give a fuck what happens to the first expedition, I'm washing myself out and this final exercise will go right on without me. I'm not going to go crazy from lack of sleep just because some brass-hat thinks superrealism is the answer. If they refuse to stop the exercise when I tell them to, why then it will be murder."

He was out of his bunk before Tony could say anything and scratching at the control board. The Emergency button was there as always, but they didn't know if it was connected this time. Or even if it were connected, if anyone would answer. Hal pushed it and kept pushing it. They both looked at the speaker, holding their breaths.

"The dirty rotten . . . they're not going to answer the call." Hall barely breathed the words.

Then the speaker rasped to life and the cold voice of Colonel Stegham filled the tiny room.

"You know the conditions of this exercise—so your reasons for calling had better be pretty good. What are they?"

Hal grabbed the microphone, half-complaining, half-pleading, the words poured out in a torrent. As soon as he started Tony knew it would not be any good. He knew just how Stegham would react to the complaints. While Hal was still pleading the speaker cut him off.

"That's enough. Your explanation doesn't warrant any change in the original plan. You are on your own and you're going to have to stay that way. I'm cutting this emergency connection permanently. Don't attempt to contact me again until the exercise is over."

The click of the opening circuit was as final as death.

Hal sat dazed, tears on his cheeks. It wasn't until he stood up that Tony realized they were tears of anger. With a single pull, Hal yanked the mike loose and heaved it through the speaker grille.

"Wait until this is over, Colonel, and I can get your pudgy neck between my hands." He whirled towards Tony. "Get out the medical kit. I'll show that idiot he's not the only one who can play boyscout with his damned exercises.''

There were four morphine styrettes in the kit; he grabbed one out, broke the seal and jabbed it against his arm. Tony didn't try to stop him, in fact, he agreed with him completely. Within a few minutes, Hal was slumped over the table snoring deeply. Tony picked him up and dropped him onto his bunk.

Hal slept almost twenty hours and when he woke some of the madness and exhaustion was gone from his eyes. Neither of them mentioned what had happened. Hal marked the days remaining on the bulkhead and carefully rationed the remaining morphine. He was getting about one night's sleep in three, but it seemed to be enough.

They had four days left to blast off when Tony found the first Martian life. It was something about the size of a cat that crouched in the lee of the ship. He called to Hal who came over and looked at it.

"That's a beauty," he said, "but nowhere near as good as the one I had on my second trip. I found this ropy thing that oozed a kind of glue. Contrary to regulations—I was curious as hell—I dissected the thing. It was a beauty, wheels and springs and gears, Stegham's technicians do a good job. I really got chewed out for opening the thing, though. Why don't we just leave this one where it is?"

For a moment Tony almost agreed—then changed his mind.

"That's probably just what they want. So let's finish the game their way. I'll watch it, you get one of the empty ration cartons.''

Hal reluctantly agreed and climbed into the ship. The outer door swung slowly and ground into place. Disturbed by the vibration, the thing darted out towards Tony. He gasped and stepped back before he remembered it was only a robot.

"Those technicians really have exotic imaginations," he mumbled.

The thing started to run by him and he put his foot on some of its legs to hold it. There were plenty of legs; it was like a small-bodied spider surrounded by a thousand unarticulated legs. They moved in undulating waves like a millipede's and dragged the misshapen body across the sand. Tony's boot crunched on the legs, tearing some off. The rest held.

Being careful to keep his hand away from the churning legs, he bent over and picked up a dismembered limb. It was hard and covered with spines on the bottom side. A milky fluid was dripping from the torn end.

"Realism," he said to himself. "Those techs sure believe in realism."

And then the thought hit him. A horribly impossible thought that froze the breath in his throat. The thoughts whirled round and round and he knew they were wrong because they were so incredible. Yet he had to find out, even if it meant ruining their mechanical toy.

Keeping his foot carefully on the thing's legs, he slipped the sharpened table knife out of his pouch and bent over. With a single, swift motion he stabbed.

"What the devil are you doing?" Hal asked, coming up behind him. Tony couldn't answer and he couldn't move. Hal walked around him and looked down at the thing on the ground.

It took him a second to understand; then he screamed.

"It's alive? It's bleeding and there are no gears inside. It can't be alive—if it is we're not on Earth at all—we're on Mars!" He began to run, then fell down, screaming.

Tony thought and acted at the same time. He knew he only had one chance. If he missed they'd both be dead. Hal would kill them both in his madness. He rolled the sobbing man onto his back. Balling his fist, he let swing as hard as he could at the spot just under Hal's breastplate. There was just the thin fabric of the suit here and that spot was right over the big nerve ganglion of the solar plexus. The thud of the blow hurt his hand—but Hal was silenced. Putting his hands under the other's arms, he dragged him into the ship.

Hal started to come to after Tony had stripped him and laid him on the bunk. It was impossible to hold him down with one hand and press the freeze cycling button at the same time. He concentrated on holding Hal's one leg still while he pushed the button. The crazed man had time to hit Tony three times before the needle lanced home into his ankle. He dropped back with a sigh and Tony got groggily to his feet. The manual actuator on the frozen sleep had been provided for any medical emergency so the patient could survive until the doctors could work on him back at base. It had proven its value.

Then the same unreasoning terror hit him.

If the beast were real then Mars was real.

This was no training exercise—this was it. That sky outside wasn't a painted atmosphere, it was the real sky of Mars.

He was alone as no man had ever been alone before, on a planet millions of miles from his world.

He was shouting as he dogged home the outer airlock door, an animal-like howl of a lost beast. He had barely enough control left to get to his bunk and throw the switch above it. The hypodermic was made of good steel so it went right through the fabric of his pressure suit. He was just reaching for the hypo arm to break it off when he dropped off into the blackness.

This time, he was slow to open his eyes. He was afraid he would see the riveted hull of the ship above his head. It was the white ceiling of the hospital, though, and he let the captive air out of his lungs. When he turned his head he saw Colonel Stegham sitting by the bed.

"Did we make it?" Tony asked. It was more of a statement than a question.

"You made it, Tony. Both of you made it. Hal is awake here in the other bed."

There was something different about the colonel's voice and it took Tony an instant to recognize it. It was the first time he had ever heard the colonel talk with any emotion other than anger.

"The first trip to Mars. You can imagine what the papers are saying about it. More important, Tech says the specimens and readouts you brought back are beyond price. When did you find out it wasn't an exercise?"

"The twenty-fourth day. We found some kind of Martian animal. I suppose we were pretty stupid not to have stumbled onto it before that."

Tony's voice had an edge of bitterness.

"Not really. Every part of your training was designed

to keep you from finding out. We were never certain if we would have to send the men without their knowledge, there was always that possibility. Psych was sure that the disorientation and separation from Earth would cause a breakdown. I could never agree with them."

"They were right," Tony said, trying to keep the memory of fear out of his voice.

"We know now they were right, though I fought them at the time. Psych won the fight and we programmed the whole trip over on their say-so. I doubt if you appreciate it, but we went to a tremendous amount of work to convince you two that you were still in the training program."

"Sorry to put you to all that trouble," Hal said coldly. The colonel flushed a little, not at the words but at the loosely reined bitterness that rode behind them. He went on as if he hadn't heard.

"Those two conversations you had over the emergency phone were, of course, taped and the playback concealed in the ship so there would be no time lag. Psych scripted them on the basis of fitting any need and apparently they worked. The second one was supposed to be the final touch of realism, in case you should start being doubtful. Then we used a variation of deep freeze that suspends about ninety-nine per cent of the body processes; it hasn't been revealed or published yet. This along with anticoagulents in the razor cut on Tony's chin covered the fact that so much time had passed."

"What about the ship?" Hal asked. "We saw it—and it was only half-completed."

"Dummy," the colonel said. "Put there for the public's benefit and all foreign intelligence services. Real one had been finished and tested weeks earlier. Getting the crew was the difficult part. What I said about no team finishing a practice exercise was true. You two men had the best records and were our best bets.

"We'll never have to do it this way again, though. Psych says that the next crews won't have that trouble; they'll be reinforced by the psychological fact that someone else was there before them. They won't be facing the complete unknown."

The colonel sat chewing his lip for a moment, then forced out the words he had been trying to say since Tony and Hal had regained consciousness.

"I want you to understand . . . both of you . . . that I would rather have gone myself than pull that kind of thing on you. I know how you must feel. Like we pulled some kind of a . . ."

"Interplanetary practical joke," Tony said. He didn't smile when he said it.

"Yes, something like that," the colonel rushed on. "I guess it was a lousy trick—but don't you see, we had to? You two were the only ones left, every other man had washed out. It had to be you two, and we had to do it the safest way.

"And only myself and three other men know what was done; what really happened on the trip. No one else will ever know about it, I can guarantee you that."

Hal's voice was quiet, but cut through the room like a sharp knife.

"You can be sure Colonel, that we won't be telling anybody about it."

When Colonel Stegham left, he kept his head down because he couldn't bring himself to see the look in the eyes of the first two explorers of Mars.

AT LAST, THE TRUE STORY OF FRANKENSTEIN

Und here, before your very eyes, is the very same monster built by my much admired great-great grandfather, Victor Frankenstein, built by him from pieces of corpses out of the dissecting rooms, stolen parts of bodies freshly buried in the grave, und even 'chunks of animals from the slaughterhouse. Now look!" The tailcoated man on the platform swung his arm out in a theatrical gesture and the heads of the close-packed crowd below swung to follow it. The dusty curtains flapped aside and the monster stood there, illuminated from above by a sickly green light.

There was a concerted gasp from the crowd and a shiver of motion.

In the front row, pressed against the rope barrier, Dan Bream mopped his face with a soggy handkerchief and smiled. It wasn't such a bad monster, considering that this was a cheapjack carnival playing the small town southern circuit. It had a deadwhite skin, undampened by sweat even in this steambath of a tent, glazed eyes, stitches and seams showing where the face had been

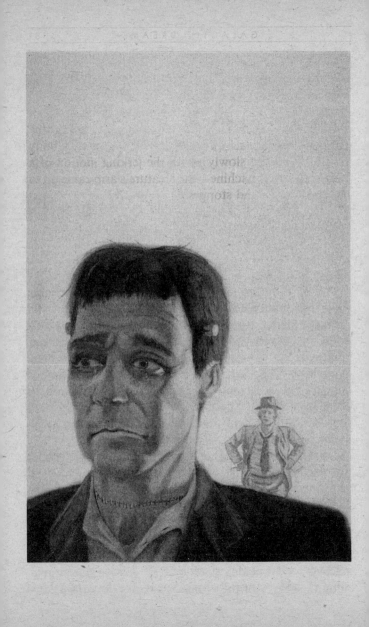

patched together. Plus the two metal plugs projecting from the temples just like in the movie.

"Raise your right arm!" Victor Frankenstein the fifth commanded, his brusque German accent giving the words a Prussian air of authority. The monster's body did not move but slowly—with the jerking motion of a badly operating machine—the creature's arm came up to shoulder height and stopped.

"This monster, built from pieces from the dead, cannot die, und if a piece gets too worn out I simply stitch on a new shtick with the secret formula passed down from father to son from my great-great grandfather. It cannot die nor feel pain, as you can see."

This time the gasp was even louder and some of the audience turned away while others watched with eager eyes. The barker had produced a foot long and wickedly sharp needle—which he then pushed firmly through the monster's biceps until it protruded on both sides. No blood stained it and the creature made no motion, as though completely unaware that anything had been done to its flesh.

". . . impervious to pain, extremes of heat and cold, possessing the strength of ten men . . ."

Behind him the voice droned on, but Dan Bream had had enough. He had seen the performance three times before, which was more than enough times for him to find out all he needed to know. It was incredibly hot; if he stayed in the tent another minute, he would melt. The exit was close by and he pushed through the gaping, pallid audience and out into the humid dusk. It wasn't much cooler outside. Life borders on the unbearable along the shores of the Gulf of Mexico in August; Pan-

ama City, Florida, was no exception. Dan headed for the
nearest air-conditioned beer joint and sighed with relief
as the chill atmosphere closed around his steaming garments. The beer bottle frosted instantly with condensa-
tion, as did the heavy glass stein, cold from the freezer.
The first big swallow cut a path straight down to his
stomach. He took the beer over to one of the straight-
backed wooden booths, wiped the table off with a hand-
ful of paper napkins and flopped onto the bench. From
the inner pocket of his jacket he took some folded sheets
of yellow copy paper now slightly soggy, and spread
them before him. After adding some lines to the scribbled
notes he stuffed them back into his jacket and took a long
pull on his beer.

Dan was halfway through his second bottle when the
barker, who called himself Frankenstein the Fifth, came
in. His stage personality had vanished along with the
frock coat and monocle; the Prussian haircut now looked
like a common crewcut.

"You've got a great act," Dan called out cheerfully as
he waved the man over. "Will you join me for a drink?"

"Don't mind if I do," Frankenstein answered in the
pure nasal vowels of New York City, the German accent
having disappeared along with the monocle. "And see if
they have a Schlitz or a Bud or anything beside local
swamp water."

He settled into the booth while Dan went for the beers
and groaned when he saw the labels on the bottles.

"At least it's cold," he said, shaking salt into his to
make it foam, then half drained the stein in a long deep
swallow.

"I noticed you out there in front of the clems for most

of the shows today. Do you like the act or you a carny buff?"

"It's a good act. I'm a newsman, name's Dan Bream."

"Always pleased to meet the Press, Dan. Publicity is the life of show business, as the man said. I'm Stanley Arnold: call me Stan."

"Then Frankenstein is just your stage name?"

"What else? You act kinda dim for a reporter, are you sure?" He waved away the Press card that Dan pulled from his breast pocket. "No, I believe you, Dan. But you gotta admit the question was a little on the rube side. I bet you even think that I have a real monster in there!"

"Well, you must admit that he looks authentic. The skin stitched together that way, those plugs in his head."

"Held on with spirit gum and the embroidery is drawn on with eyebrow pencil. That's show business for you, all illusion. But I'm happy to hear that the act even looked real to an experienced reporter like yourself. What paper did you say you were with?"

"No paper, the news syndicate. I caught your act about six months ago and became interested. Did a little checking when I was in Washington, then followed you down here. You don't really want me to call you Stan, do you? Stein might be closer. After all, Victor Frankenstein is the name on your naturalization papers."

"Tell me more," Frankenstein said in a voice suddenly cold and emotionless.

Dan riffled through the yellow sheets. "Yes . . . here it is, from the official records. Frankenstein, Victor, born Geneva, Switzerland, arrived in the U.S. in 1938, and more of the same."

"Come on guy—the next thing you'll be telling me is

that my monster is real!" Frankenstein smiled, but only
with his lips, a quick and insincere movement.

"I'm betting that it is. No yogi training or hypnotism
or such can make a man as indifferent to pain as that
thing is—and as terribly strong. I want the real story, the
truth for a change!"

"Do you . . .?" Frankenstein asked in a cold voice and
for a long moment the air filled with tension. Then he
laughed and clapped the reporter on the arm. "All right
Dan, I'll give it to you. You are a persistent devil and a
good reporter and it is the least you deserve. But first you
must get us some more drink, something that is a measurable degree stronger than this execrable beer." His New
York accent had disappeared as easily as had his German
one; he spoke English now with skill and perfection,
without a recognizable regional accent.

Dan gathered their empty glasses. "It'll have to be
beer—this is a dry county."

"Nonsense! This is America, the land that raises hands
in horror at the foreign conception of double-think—yet
practices it with an efficiency that sets the Old World to
shame. Bay County may be officially dry but the law has
many itchy palms. Under that counter you will find a
reasonable supply of a clear liquid that glories in the
name of White Mule and is reputed to have a kick of the
same magnitude as its cognate beast. If you are still in
doubt you will see a framed federal liquor license on the
far wall, legitimatizing this endeavor in the eyes of the
national government. Simply place a five dollar bank
note on the bar, say Mountain Dew, and do not expect
any change."

After they both had enjoyed their first sips of the corn

likker, Victor Frankenstein sighed happily and lapsed into a friendly mood.

"Call me Vic, Dan. I want us to be friends. Because I'm going to tell you a story that few have heard before, a story that is astounding but true. True, mark that word, not a hodgepodge of distortions and half-truths—or outright ignorance like that vile book produced by Mary Godwin. Oh how my father ever regretted meeting that woman and, in moment of weakness, confiding in her the secret of some of his original lines of research. . . ."

"Just a minute," Dan broke in. "You mentioned the truth but I can't swallow this guff. Mary Godwin Shelley wrote *Frankenstein; or, The Modern Prometheus* in 1818. Which would make you and your father so old . . ."

"Please, Dan, no interruptions. I mentioned my father's researches, in the plural you will note. All of them devoted to the secrets of life. The Monster, as it has come to be called, was just one of his works. Longevity was what he was really interested in, and he did live to be a very, very old age. As will I. Nor will I stretch your credulity any further at this moment by mentioning the year of my birth. Let us press on. That Mary Godwin! She and the poet were living together at this period, they had not married as yet, and this fact permitted my father to hope that the lovely Mary might someday find him not unattractive. You must understand that he was smitten, was quite taken by her. Well, you can easily imagine the end. She made notes of everything he told her, then discarded him and used the notes to construct her despicable book. Her errors are legion, listen. . . ." He leaned across the booth and once again clapped Dan on the shoulder in a hearty way. It was an intimate gesture that

the reporter did not particularly enjoy. Still, he did not
complain. Nor would he as long as the man kept on
talking.

"Firstly she made Papa a Swiss; he used to tear his hair
out at the thought, since ours is a good old Bavarian
family with a noble and ancient lineage. Then she had
him attending the University of Ingolstadt in Ingolstadt—when every schoolboy knows that it was moved
to Landshut in 1800. And father's personality, what
crimes she committed there! In this libelous volume he is
depicted as a weeping and ineffectual man—when in reality he was a tower of strength and determination. And if
this isn't enough, she completely misunderstood the
meaning of his experiments. Her gimcrack collection of
cast-off parts, sewn together to make an artificial man is
completely ludicrous. She was so carried away by the
legends of Talos and the Golem that she misinterpreted
my father's work and cast it into that ancient mold.
Father did not construct an artificial man, he re-activated
a dead man! That, you must understand, is the measure
of his genius. He had traveled for years in the darkest
reaches of the African jungle, learning the lore of the
creation of the zombie. He regularized the knowledge
and improved upon it until he had surpassed all of his
aboriginal teachers. Raise the dead, that is what he could
do. That was his secret—and how can it be kept a secret
in the future, Mr. Dan Bream?"

With these last words Victor Frankenstein's eyes
opened wide and a strange light seemed to glow in their
depths. Dan pulled back instinctively, then relaxed. He
was in no danger here in this brightly lit room with men
on all sides of them.

"Afraid, Dan? You should not be." Victor smiled and reached out and patted Dan on the shoulder once again.

"What was that?" Dan asked, startled at the tiny brief pain in his shoulder.

"Why, nothing—absolutely nothing—except this." Frankenstein smiled again, but the smile had changed subtly and no longer contained even the slightest trace of any humor. He opened his hand to reveal a small hypodermic needle, its plunger pushed down and its barrel empty.

"Remain seated," he said quietly when Dan started to rise. Dan's muscles instantly relaxed and he sat back down horrified.

"What have you done to me?"

"Very little. The injection is harmless. A hypnotic drug the effect of which will wear off in a few hours. But until then you will not have much will of your own. So you will sit and hear me out. Drink some beer as well since we don't want you to be thirsty."

Horrified, Dan was a helpless onlooker as, of its own volition, his hand raised and poured a measure of beer down his throat.

"Now concentrate Dan, think of the significance of my statement. The so-called Frankenstein monster is no stitched-up collection of scraps, but a good honest zombie. A dead man who can walk but not talk, obey but not think. Animate—but still quite dead. Poor old Charley is a zombie, the creature whom you watched going through his act on the platform. But Charley is just about worn out. Since he is dead he cannot replace the body cells that are destroyed during the normal wear and tear of the day. Why the fellow is like an animated pincushion from

the act, holes everywhere. His feet are terrible, not a toe
left, they keep breaking off when he walks too fast. I
think it's time to retire Charley. He has had a long life,
and a long death. Stand up Dan."

In spite of his mind crying No! No! Dan rose slowly to
his feet. Victor smiled and nodded approval.

"Aren't you interested in what Charley used to do
before he became a sideshow monster? You should be,
Dan. Old Charley was a reporter—just like you. And he
uncovered what he thought was a really good story. Like
you, he didn't realize the importance of what he had
discovered and talked to me about it. You reporters are
very inquisitive—I must show you my scrapbook one
day, it's simply filled with Press cards. Show it to you
before you die of course. You wouldn't be able to appreciate it afterwards. Now come along."

Dan walked after him, into the hot night, screaming
inside in a haze of terror, yet walking quietly and silently
down the street.

THE ROBOT
WHO WANTED
TO KNOW

That was the trouble with Filer 13B-445-K, he wanted to know things that he had just no business knowing. Things that no robot should be interested in—much less investigate. But Filer was a very different type of Robot.

The trouble with the blonde in tier 22 should have been warning enough for him. He had hummed out of the stack room with a load of books, and was cutting through tier 22 when he saw her bending over for a volume on the bottom shelf.

As he passed behind her he slowed down, then stopped a few yards farther on. He watched her intently, a strange glint in his metallic eyes.

As the girl bent over her short skirt rode up to display an astonishing length of nylon-clad leg. That it was a singularly attractive leg should have been of no interest to a robot—yet it was. He stood there, looking, until the blonde turned suddenly and noticed his fixed attention.

"If you were human, buster," she said, "I would slap

your face. But since you are a robot, I would like to
know what your little photon-filled eyes find so interesting?"

Without a microsecond's hesitation, Filer answered,
"Your seam is crooked." Then he turned and buzzed
away.

The blonde shook her head in wonder, straightened
the offending stocking, and chalked up another credit to
the honor of electronics.

She would have been very surprised to find out what
Filer had been looking at. He had been staring at her leg.
Of course he hadn't lied when he answered her—since he
was incapable of lying—but he had been looking at a lot
more than the crooked seam. Filer was facing a problem
that no other robot had ever faced before.

Love, romance, and sex were fast becoming a passion-
ate interest for him.

That this interest was purely academic goes without
saying, yet it was still an interest. It was the nature of his
work that first aroused his curiosity about the realm of
Venus.

A Filer is an amazingly intelligent robot and there
aren't very many being manufactured. You will find
them only in the greatest libraries, dealing with only the
largest and most complex collections. To call them simply librarians is to demean all librarians and to call their
work simple. Of course very little intelligence is required
to shelve books or stamp cards, but this sort of work has
long been handled by robots that are little more than
programmed computers on wheels. The cataloging of
human information has always been an incredibly com-

plex task. The Filer robots were the ones who finally
inherited this job. It rested easier on their metallic shoulders than it ever had on the rounded ones of human
librarians.

Besides having a very complete and easily accessible
memory, Filer had other attributes that are usually connected with the human brain. Abstract connections for
one thing. If he was asked for books on one subject, he
could think of related books in other subjects that might
be referred to. He could take a suggestion, pyramid it
into a category, then produce tactile results in the form
of a mountain of books.

These traits are usually confined to homo sapiens.
They are the things that pulled him that last, long step
above his animal relatives. If Filer was more human than
other robots, he had only his builders to blame.

He blamed no one—he was just interested. All Filers
are interested, they are designed that way. Another Filer,
9B-367-0, librarian at the university in Tashkent, had
turned his interest to language due to the immense
amount of material at his disposal. He spoke thousands
of languages and dialects, all that he could find texts on,
and enjoyed a great reputation in linguistic circles. That
was because of his library. Filer 13B, he of the interest in
girls' legs, labored in the dust filled corridors of New
Washington. In addition to all the gleaming new mi-
crofiles, he had access to tons of ancient printed-on-
paper books that dated back for centuries.

Filer had found his interest in the novels of that by-
gone time. At first he was confused by all the references

to love and romance, as well as the mental and physical suffering that seemed to accompany them. He could find no satisfactory or complete definition of the terms and was intrigued. Intrigue led to interest and finally absorption. Unknown to the world at large, he became an authority on Love.

Very early in his interest, Filer realized that this was the most delicate of all human institutions. He therefore kept his researches a secret and the only records he had were in the capacious memory circuits of his brain. Just about the same time he discovered that he could do research *in vivo* to supplement the facts in his books. This happened when he found a couple locked in embrace in the zoology section.

Quickly stepping back into the shadows, Filer had turned up the gain on his audio pickup. The resulting dialogue he heard was dull to say the least. A gray and wasted shadow of the love lyrics he knew from his books. This comparison was interesting and enlightening.

After that he listened to male-female conversations whenever he had the opportunity. He also tried to look at women from the viewpoint of men, and vice versa. This is what had led him to the lower-limb observation in tier 22.

It also led him to his ultimate folly.

A researcher sought his aid a few weeks later and fumbled out a thick pile of reference notes. A card slid from the notes and fell unnoticed to the floor. Filer picked it up and handed it back to the man who put it away with mumbled thanks. After the man had been

supplied with the needed books and gone, Filer sat back
and reread the card. He had only seen it for a split
second, and upside down at that, but that was all he
needed. The image of the card was imprinted forever in
his memory. Filer mused over the card and the first glim-
merings of an idea assailed him.

The card had been an invitation to a masquerade ball.
He was well acquainted with this type of entertainment—
it was stock-in-trade for his dusty novels. People went to
them disguised as various romantic figures.

Why couldn't a robot go, disguised as people?

Once the idea was fixed in his head there was no driving it out. It was an un-robot thought and a completely
un-robot action. Filer had a glimmering of the first time
that he was breaking down the barrier between himself
and the mysteries of romance. This only made him more
eager to go. And of course he did.

There was no possible way to purchase a costume, but
there was no problem in obtaining some ancient curtains
from one of the storerooms. A book on sewing taught
him the technique and a plate from a book gave him the
design for his costume. It was predestined that he go as
a cavalier.

With a finely ground pen point he printed an exact
duplicate of the invitation on heavy card stock. His mask
was part face and part mask, it offered no barrier to his
talent or technology. Long before the appointed date he
was ready. The last days were filled with browsing
through stories about other masquerade balls and learning the latest dance steps.

So enthused was he by the idea, that he never stopped

to ponder the strangeness of what he was doing. He was just a scientist studying a species of animal. Man. Or rather woman.

The night finally arrived and he left the library late with what looked like a package of books, and of course wasn't. No one noticed him enter the patch of trees on the library grounds. If they had, they would certainly never have connected him with the elegant gentleman who swept out of the far side a few moments later. Only the empty wrapping paper bore mute evidence of the disguise.

Filer's manner in his new personality was all that might be expected of a superior robot who has studied a role to perfection. He swept up the stairs to the hall three at a time, and tendered his invitation with a flourish. Once inside he headed straight for the bar and threw down three glasses of champagne, right through a plastic tube to a tank in his thorax. Only then did he let his eye roam over the assembled beauties. It was a night for love.

And of all the women in the room, there was only one he had eyes for. Filer could see instantly that she was the belle of the ball and the one he must approach. Could he do anything else in memory of the 50,000 heroes of those long-forgotten books?

Carol Ann van Damm was bored as usual. Her face was disguised, but no mask could hide the generous contours of her bosom and flanks. All her usual suitors were there, dancing attendance behind their dominoes, lusting after her youth and her father's money. It was all too familiar and she had trouble holding back her yawns.

Until the pack was courteously but irrevocably pushed aside by the wide shoulders of the stranger. He was a lion among wolves as he swept through them and head her.

"This is our dance," he said in a deep voice rich with meaning. Almost automatically she took the proffered hand, unable to resist this man with the strange gleam in his eyes. In a moment they were waltzing and it was heaven. His muscles were like steel yet he was light and graceful as a god.

"Who are you," she whispered.

"Your prince, come to take you away from all this," he murmured in her ear.

"You talk like a fairy tale," she laughed.

"This is a fairy tale, and you are the heroine."

His words struck fire in her brain and she felt the thrill of an electric current sweep through her. It had, but it was just a temporary short circuit. While his lips murmured the words she had wanted to hear all her life into her ear, his magic feet led her through the great doors onto the balcony. Once there words blended with action and hot lips burned against hers. 102 degrees to be exact, that was what the thermostat was set at.

"Please," she breathed, weak with this new passion, "I must sit down." He sat next to her, her hands in his soft yet vise-like grip. They talked the words that only lovers know until a burst of music drew her attention.

"Midnight," she breathed. "Time to unmask, my love." Her mask dropped off, but he of course did nothing. "Come, come," she said. "You must take your mask off too."

It was a command and of course as a robot he had to obey. With a flourish he pulled off his face.

Carol Ann screamed first, then instantly burned with anger.

"What sort of scheme is this, you animated tin can? Answer."

"It was love, dear one. Love that brought me here tonight and sent me to your arms." The answer was true enough, though Filer couched it in the terms of his disguise.

When the soft words of her darling came out of the harsh mouth of the electronic speaker Carol Ann screamed again. She knew she had been made a fool of.

"Who sent you here like this, answer. What is the meaning of this disguise, answer, ANSWER! ANSWER! you articulated pile of cams and rods!"

Filer tried to sort out the questions and answer them one at a time, but she gave him no time to speak.

"It's the filthiest trick of all time, sending you here disguised as a man. You're a robot. A nothing. A two-legged IBM machine with a victrola attached. Making believe you're man when you're nothing but a robot."

Suddenly Filer was on his feet, the words crackling mechanically from his speaker.

"I am a robot."

The gentle voice of love was gone and replaced by one of mechanical despair. Thought chased thought through the whirling electronic circuits of his brain and they were all the same thought.

I'm a robot—a robot—I must have forgotten I was a robot. What can a robot be doing here with a woman—a robot cannot kiss a woman—a woman cannot love a

robot yet she said she loved me—yet I'm a robot—
a robot . . .

With a mechanical shudder he turned his back on the
girl and clanked away. With each step his steel fingers
plucked at clothes and plastic flesh until they tore free in
shards and pieces. Fragments of cloth marked his trail
away from the woman, and within a hundred paces he
was as steel naked as the day he was built. Through the
garden down to the street he went, the thoughts in his
head going in ever tighter circles.

It was uncontrolled feedback and soon his body followed his brain. His legs went faster, his motors whirled
more rapidly, and the central lubrication pump in his
thorax churned like a mad thing.

Then, with a single metallic screech, he raised both
arms and plunged forward. His head hit a corner of a
stair and the granite point thrust into the thin casing.
Metal ground to metal and all the complex circuits that
made up his were instantly discharged.

Robot Filer 13B-445-K was quite dead.

That was how the report read that the mechanic sent
in the following day. Not dead, but permanently im-
paired, unrepairable, to be disposed of. Yet, strangely
enough, that wasn't what this same man had said when
he examined the metallic corpse.

A second mechanic had helped in the examination. It
was he who had spun off the bolts and pulled out the
damaged lubrication pump.

"Here's the trouble," he had announced. "Malfunc-
tion in the pump. Piston broke, jammed the pump, the

knees locked from lack of oil—then the robot fell and shorted out its brains."

The first mechanic wiped grease off his hands and examined the faulty pump. Then looked from it to the gaping hole in the chest.

."You could almost say he died of a broken heart."

They both laughed and he threw the pump into the corner with all the other cracked, dirty, broken and discarded machinery.

BILL, THE GALACTIC HERO'S HAPPY HOLIDAY

I t was a big bribe, a full bottle of DrainO—the Drunk-
ard's Delight, 180 proof and strong enough to etch
glass. But knowing this man's Army—or any Man's
Army—Bill did not slip it to the Duty Sergeant until
he had actually seen his name posted on the leave roster.

This was it! His first R&R ever. His lips lifted in an
unaccustomed smile, a drop of saliva on each fang, as he
read his orders.

> Now hear this. At 0324 hours you will be taken in
> the company of other R&Rs to the luxurious Holi-
> day Island of Anthrax where you will Enjoy sun,
> sand, etc. Not enjoying is punishable by death. . . .

His eyes were so misted with simple pleasure that he
could read no further. He would enjoy the sun and
sand—and even learn to like the etc.

Promptly at 0324 the following morning nothing hap-

pened, for this was the military way. Bill, and the other lucky Troopers, sat buckled into their knobbed-steel seats in the hover-jumper for over two hours until, prompted by some secret signal, the pilot started the engines and the hovercraft, lifted by its mighty fans, floated across the beach to the ocean beyond.

And hurtled a hundred feet into the air—and crashed back to the sea.

"Accident! We're doomed!" Bill shouted as his teeth clashed together and his head was slammed down onto his spine.

"Shut your gob, bowbhead," grated the Sergeant in the seat next to him—just as there was another horrendous collision. "Civilian hovercraft hover. This is the military version that jumps as well. To dodge enemy fire."

"And crush everyone inside at the same time?"

"That's right, bowb-boy. You're learning."

After a lifetime of soaring and crashing there was a sudden stillness. Broken only by the moans of the castrated, crunched and crumbled Troopers.

"Disembark!" the loudspeakers grated. "Last one off gets latrine duty for the week."

Sobbing and moaning the happy holiday makers crawled and stumbled to the exit, fought their way free of this hideous form of transport. Staggered and fell onto the sandy shore.

"This sand is black," Bill mumbled.

"Of course it is," the Sergeant said sadistically. "Because this is a volcanic island and lava is black. Fall in for roll call!"

As punctuation to his words there was an orgasmic

rumble in the ground, which shook beneath their feet like
a dog scratching fleas, and they looked in horror as the
top of a nearby mountain spewed out smoke and a few
clods of flying stone. "Are we getting our R&R on an
active volcano?" Bill asked.

"Where else in the military," the Sergeant said not
unreasonably. "Shout out when you hear your name.
Aardvark . . ."

They stood in the burning tropical sun—that is those
who didn't collapse with heatstroke—until the Sergeant
reached Zzowski. Only then did they march in staggering
formation into the jungle.

It was a long climb up to the R&R barracks. Made
even longer by the truckloads of officers that roared by
them, laughing gaily, waving emptying bottles and giving
them the finger. They could only plod on in insulting
silence.

It was dusk before they reached the summit. Here the
road split; a sign reading OFFICERS ONLY pointed to the
right. Ahead of them fumaroles steamed out clouds of
sulfur dioxide and other poisonous chemicals. There was
still enough light to reveal that the trade winds blew the
clouds off to the left. Shuffling, wheezing, coughing, crying they found the way to their holiday bungalows,
downwind from the volcano of course, and dropped onto
the rock-hard bunks.

"Gee this is fun!" Bill said, smiling through his tears,
then lifted his arm to ward off the flying boots that came
his way.

Even these hardened Troopers found it difficult to fall
asleep with the seismic rumblings and acrid VOG, Volcanic Smog. But if they hadn't learned to sleep under

these, or worse, conditions they would all have been long-since dead of fatigue. Within minutes the zizzing of snores, and death-rattles of acid-eaten throats, made live the night. Until the lights flashed on and the sergeant burst through the door bellowing loudly.

"An attack! A Chinger attack!"

They groaned awake, groped for their boots, until the sergeant added, "They're attacking the officers' quarters!"

Groans were replaced by cheers as they hurled their boots away and climbed back into the sack. Only to be stirred out again as the sergeant shot holes in the ceiling.

"I share the feeling," he growled empathetically. "But they may hit us next. To arms."

This reasoned argument, appealing to their sense of survival—not the officers—sent them to the gun lockers.

Bill, dressed only in natty orange underpants and boots, grabbed up an ion rifle, checked that it was fully charged, then joined the others on the porch to enjoy the fun. Explosions and screams of pain penetrated the clouds of drifting VOG.

"Hear that? Must of got a dozen of the bowbers that time!"

"And I almost volunteered for OCS!"

It was good, clean fun and Bill, smiling with heartfelt pleasure, wandered out onto the grass to see if he could get a better view of the entertainment.

"Psst, Bill—over here," someone whispered from behind the bushes.

"Who's that?" he said suspiciously. "I don't know anyone here."

"But I know you, Bill. We were shipmates on the

battleship *Forniqueteur,* the grand old lady of the fleet."

"So what?"

"So I got a bottle of Plutonian Panther Pee I don't want to share with the others."

"Good buddy! Yes, I do remember you now!"

Bill walked around the bush and there was just enough moonlight filtering through the clouds of gunge for him to make out the tiny form of a Chinger standing there.

"To arms!" Bill cried, lifting his rifle.

A small but powerful hand pulled it from his grasp. The Chinger bounded high and a hard fist cracked Bill's jaw, dropping him, half-stunned, to the ground.

"Come on, Bill—you remember me. I've saved your life more than once."

"Bgr? Bgr the Chinger?"

"You got that in one—after all, how many Chingers do you know? We staged this raid as a diversion—"

"You mean you're not killing the officers?" he asked, unhappily.

"Of course we are. Now shut up and let me finish. A diversion so I could get through to you. We need your help. . . ."

"Do you think that I am a traitor to the human race!"

"Yes. You are a trained Trooper who will do anything to save his own hide. Right?"

"Right. But traitoring doesn't come cheap. What's the pay?"

"A lifetime subscription to the Booze of the Month Club. Their motto—A barrel on the first means you'll never die of thirst. There is no mention, however, of hobnailed livers."

"Done. Who do I have to kill?"

"Nobody. And you don't have to be a traitor either. That was just my little trap to expose what bowbheads you humans are. Now let's get out of here before the diversion ends."

Bgr led the way to an ornamental fountain crowned by an immense fish spewing out water. The water stopped when he twisted the fish's tail and a door opened in its side.

"In," Bgr ordered.

"What is it? A miniature spaceship disguised as a fountain?"

"Well it's not a subway train. Move—before we're spotted."

A sudden spattering of bullets at his heels sent Bill diving through the opening. He was bashed flat by acceleration and when he finally struggled to his feet Bgr was at the controls; stars punctured the darkness outside the window. The Chinger stabbed down a button and the stars began to shrink as the spacer's Bloater Drive fired up.

"Good," Bgr said, spinning around in his chair. "Have a cigar and I'll tell you what's up."

Bill took one of the proffered cigars and lit it. Bgr ate the rest of them and belched contentedly.

"Different metabolisms. What we are on is a rescue mission."

"Kidnapped maidens?"

"Hardly. A Chinger of course. Trapped in his ship when the engines were shot out. He's very important to us—"

"Why?"

"If I told you that you would sell him out to the

highest bidder. Let's just say important. Spring him and you are drunk for life."

"Why can't you do it yourself?"

"For the simple reason, bowb-brain, that I am not human. Mgr, which happens to be his name, is imprisoned on the highly militarized planet of Parra'Noya. Any disguise would be instantly penetrated. You, however, are disgustingly human and can boldly go where we can't."

"I want an advance on my salary," Bill said, beginning to be worried.

"Why not. You can travel just as well smashed. Nothing could possibly improve or hinder your conversational abilities. Here."

"Here" was a suspiciously green flask of liquid labeled in an unknown language. None of which would deter a determined boozehead in search of escape. The first mouthful tasted preposterously foul and Bill could feel steam leaking out of his ears. But the more he drank the better it tasted and he was soon twanging a tusk with contentment as he slipped into oblivion.

"Disgusting. Chingers don't drink—or have BO."

The clang of mighty bells awoke Bill, groaning. It was some time before he realized that they were inside his head.

He needed both hands to pry one eye open; it clanged shut and he groaned even more loudly as the light seared and sizzled through his skull.

"Appalling," Bgr sneered as he plunged a hypodermic into Bill's arm. Whatever it was took affect almost instantly and the symptoms of the galaxy-sized hangover began to fade. As the blear faded from his eyes Bill saw a grizzled Admiral of the Fleet standing before him. He snapped to attention and saluted with his two right arms.

Surprisingly, the Admiral did the same. Much rapid blinking revealed the fact that he was looking at himself in the mirror.

"My true rank at last," he simpered, strutting and rattling his medals.

"Come off it. You aren't intelligently qualified to even make Private First Class. Now listen to instructions and try to remember them. They are very complicated. Almost as complicated as learning to be a fuse tender."

"That wasn't easy—but I did it!"

"Indeed. Listen. Your instructions have been mnemonically implanted in your subconscious. To access your orders you must say the word 'harumph' aloud."

"Is that all?"

"That's it. Do you think that you can master all the complications and pitfalls of these complex instructions?"

"Harumph." Bill said, then hooked his thumbs into his gunbelt and began to speak in resounding tones. "I say, my good man, don't you realize that you are in the presence of a Grand Admiral of the fleet. . . ."

"Un-harumph!" Bgr called out and Bill staggered back.

"Did I say that?"

"You did. The implants work. Now the battle starts."

"What battle?

"The staged battle, bowb-brain, from which you will escape in a lifeboat that will take you to Parra'Noya."

Bgr hit the communication button and the imaged form of another green, four-armed Chinger appeared on the screen.

"Tydsmnx," Bgr said.

"Mrtnzl," the other answered and vanished from the screen.

"A human like you would have to talk for five minutes to express what we said. A remarkably compact language, Chingerian."

"Doesn't sound nice."

"Who asked you? Get over to the door, because your transport of delight is here."

A crunched and burnt lifeboat drifted into view and clanged against their hull as the airlocks lined up.

"Move it!" Bgr ordered and Bill moved out of the fountain-spaceship and into the other. He strapped himself into the pilot's seat and was just reaching for the controls when Bgr's voice boomed in his ears.

"Don't touch anything, bowb-brains. This thing is remotely controlled. Have a good day—"

The Chinger's voice was wiped out by the roar of rockets as the lifeboat blasted forward. Straight into the ravening maw of a full-fledged space battle. Bill shrieked as guns and space-mines exploded and ravened on all sides.

The little rocket blasted through the engagement and out the other side—heading for the blue globe of a rapidly expanding planet. As gravity grabbed onto it the engine cut out and Bill continued to moan in terror as they dropped uncontrollably towards the clouds below.

The military base, bulging with guns and turrets, rushed towards them at an accelerating pace. But, at the last possible microsecond, the parachute snapped out and the lifeboat settled gently in the middle of a drillfield. The door ground open, Bill patted his newly-gray hair smooth, hauled his stomach up into his chest in the best military manner and stamped out.

"Hold it right there spy—or you'll be fried into dog-food!"

A snarling sentry stood outside with his heatray leveled at Bill's gut, his finger twitching on the trigger.

"Urggle!" Bill said.

"What?"

"I mean—Burble!" His skin grayed to match his hair as he realized he had forgotten the word of command!

"I say—what's going on here?" a General in full body armor said as he clanged up.

"Spacer landed, sir. This madman got out. Can't talk."

"Nonsense. Can't you see that he is an officer? Other ranks are mad, officers are eccentric." He turned to Bill and saluted. "Welcome to Parra'Noya, Admiral."

"Eeek," Bill eeked.

"Indeed," the general said, bulging his eyes, not knowing what to say, "Harumph," he finally harumphed.

"That's it!" Bill jovialated. "Harumph! Quite a pleasure to meet you General. Bit of a space battle out there. Few thousand ships destroyed, got a few of the buggers on the other side as well."

"Can't make an omelet without breaking eggs."

"Quite. I nipped into this lifeship when my battleship blew up. Now—I suggest you show me a bit of hospitality and discipline this soldier for pointing a weapon at a superior officer."

"Of course. You—give me that weapon and turn yourself in to the MPs for two years in a labor battalion.

"Dismissed."

Sobbing with despair the soldier staggered away. The officers, now good chums, headed hand in hand for the bar where they raised glasses of vintage champagne in jolly toasting.

"To your fine military planet," Bill smarmed. "Long may it reign."

"To your fine space navy—long may it destroy!"

Bill drained his glass, belched, and nodded happily as it was refilled. "This is Parra'Noya, isn't it?"

"Indeed it is."

"I seem to remember a space-o-gram that came in just before the ship exploded. Something about a prisoner you had . . ."

"That will be our captive Chinger!"

"I say—no one has ever captured a Chinger before."

"That's because no one is as militaristically sadistically warlike as we are. Like to see the bugger?"

"Is that his name?"

"Almost. I believe it is Mgr."

"Well lead on, old bean. Can I help you torture the creature or something?"

"Nice of you to offer. I'll see what can be arranged."

They finished the bottle, lit cigars, then strolled deep into the fortress. Guards clashed their weapons at attention as they passed. Electronic gates swung open and squads of troops trotted by with presented arms. Deeper and deeper they went until the metal walls gave way to damp stone. Furtive rodents rustled away and even the guards were covered with mold and spiderwebs. One last

sealed gate was unsealed and resealed and they stood
before a barred door. The guard raised his weapon in a
snappy salute and stepped aside. Bill looked in at the
Chinger chained to the wall with massive metal shackles.

"I thought they were bigger," he said.

"Big, small, green, too many arms, doesn't matter.
They are the enemy and shall be destroyed."

"Hear, hear. I say, what is that unusual weapon the
guard is holding?"

"A new invention. Shackle-ray projector. Sends out
rings of energy that enwrap the victim with unbreakable
bonds of paralyzing radiation."

"Sounds wizard. Might I see it?"

Even before permission was given Bill took hold of the
gun, Reversed it, looked down the muzzle. Reversed it
again and shot the guard and the General. They fell,
screaming and writhing into unconsciousness, wrapped
in purple flame. Bill looked through the bars at the
Chinger and spoke.

"*Grtzz?*"

"*Zimtz!* And I'm mighty glad to see you, vulgar
human bearer of succor sent by my hive-mate Bgr. You
can now un-harumph."

At this command Bill's imposed personality vanished
and his teeth began chattering with fear. "We're good as
dead! Deep in the enemy stronghold!"

"Shut up," Mgr kindly suggested as he seized his
chains and snapped them easily. "You won't see a bowby
human doing this. Or this," he added as he bent the cell
bars into loops and stepped out into the passageway.
"Did you see any robots around?"

"Why?"

"Just answer and don't try to think with your limited capacity. Robots—remember? Metal men with wheels and glass eyes."

"Yes, I think, maybe. A janitor robot down the hall."

"Perfect."

The Chinger jumped over the unconscious General and went to the control panel beside the closed portal.

"Harumph," he said as he pushed the button and the door opened a crack. Bill stamped forward and spoke through the crack.

"I say, guards, step in here for a moment."

As the door opened wider he seized up the ray gun and added some more numb bodies to the growing pile. Mgr stayed well out of sight as he said "Un-harumph." Bill vibrated and moaned with fear again.

"Knock that off or I'll leave you here for certain death and dismemberment. Do what I say and you stand a chance of getting out of here in one piece or more. Get that robot in here."

Bill moaned but went. The Chinger was his only chance.

The robot was mopping the hall but stopped when he called to it.

"You, robot, come here."

"Me robot already here," it grated with metallic stupidity.

"You—robot—put 'em down mop. Roll to big human chief."

"Me—robot—do what big chief tell it."

Clanking and muttering mechanically it rolled through the door and stopped when the Chinger jumped onto its shoulder and opened the access plate in its head.

"Klinkle!" it said as Mgr tore out handfuls of wire and machinery and threw them to the floor. When he had made enough room he climbed inside and slammed the plate closed behind him.

"Let's roll!" the revitalized robot said. "And you better Harumph again since you are pretty useless in the quivering coward persona. Say it!"

"Harumph!" Bill quavered—then took a brace. "Shall we proceed, dear nest-mate of mine? I assume you have a plan of escape."

"Indeed I do," the robot grated as it grabbed up its mop. "You lead the way and I'll roll behind you. We have to go up thirty stories to the top level. I spotted some aerial transport there when they carried me by."

The guard at the next portal widened his eyes as Bill approached. "You do know that you are being followed by a janitorbot?"

"Am I? I thought I heard a rattling."

As Bill spoke the robot rolled past him—and crashed his mop down on the guard's head. "Time for you to change persona," the Chingerbot said as it stripped off the guard's uniform. Bill nodded agreement and peeled down. Swift seconds later guard and robot rolled on. They had just reached the hellevator shaft when the alarm clanged over their heads.

"They've caught on!" Bill shouted.

"Up the Chingers!" the robot bellowed and tore open the hellevator doors. The moving ladders inside were bright red. Metal hand and human hand grabbed out as one and they were quickly whisked upward. At the top of the shaft the door opened and the soldiers outside fired their guns all at the same time.

"It's a good thing Chinger and electronic reflexes are faster than your sluggish human ones," Mgr said, slamming the doors shut an instant before the guns ravened. The metal doors glowed hot. "Let's try the floor below."

It was a race against time, a desperate bid for survival. Every man's hand was turned against them—women's as well they discovered when a gun-wielding WAAC singed their bums as they raced by.

Words cannot reveal the terrors they faced that day. The close encounters of a fourth kind, the skin of their teeth well flayed, the cliff-hangers well hung. It was only minutes but it seemed like hours before they stumbled through one last door and into the rain outside. Singed, scalded, bent and more than a little mutilated, Bill patted the sparks from his trousers while the robot raised its one remaining arm to open the plate in its head. It clanged limply to the ground as the Chinger jumped free.

"Un-harumph," Mgr said. "And, if possible, let us not do that again. Now, if you can stop clattering your teeth together in that disgusting manner, you can look about and tell me where we are."

"In the rain. . . ."

"Brilliant. The entire human race to pick from and Bgr sends me one with the intellect of a brain-dead mouse. Listen, stupid, you are human and I, as is obvious, am not. So look about and let me know where we are."

"I've never been here before."

"I know that. But bulge your eyes, make a guess. All I know about humans is what I read in reports. I may be head of the CIA, Chinger Intelligence Assessment, but I have never been on a human planet before. What's that?"

"The town garbage dump. So you're pretty high up, huh?"

"Nobody higher. I run the war and have been doing a damn fine job of it. And if you try to tell anybody who I am you'll be dead before the first word leaves your lips.

"What is garbage?"

"Things people throw out."

"Good. Let's take a look."

They skulked rapidly through the rain, from one place of concealment to the other. Finally hiding behind a heap of broken cogwheels as a rumbling sound grew louder, coming towards them.

"Peek out and look," Mgr ordered. "What is it?"

"A garbage truck. What else did you expect to find in a garbage dump?"

"How many humans in it?"

"None. It's a robot garbage truck."

"You have just made my day, simple human. Let's climb aboard."

Sodden and weary they climbed up the cab and slammed the door shut behind them.

"No humans allowed," the robot driver grated out.

"Against law, me no like, krrkkk—" It krrkked its last as Mgr tore its head off and pushed it aside.

"Drive," he said to Bill. "That is I assume you can operate this vehicle?"

"A truck's a truck," Bill said sanguinely, kicking it into gear, revving the engine—and plowing backwards into a mountain of garbage. "Though sometimes, ha-ha, it takes a second or two to work out the controls."

"Well take a second or four and try not to do that

again. We Chingers have most delicate senses of smell."

Bill fiddled with the controls and finally got them working. Put the thing into forward and rumbled out of the garbage dump. The rain was letting up and they could see the fortress behind them, green fields off to the side. Mgr peeked out of a hole he had punched in the door.

"That way—towards the jungle."

"Those are farms."

"Spare me the linguistic lesson and head for the hills. I want to be as far away from the troops as we can get before calling for help."

They rumbled on and Bill began to master the controls.

When a squad of tanks came their way he stopped and, using the extensible arms, he actually emptied some garbage cans so as not to arouse suspicion.

"Pretty good," he said proudly as the tanks vanished with a great slurping of churned-up mud.

"Would have been a lot better," Mgr sneered, "If you had got the garbage into the hole on top instead of dumping it into the street."

"It's not that easy," Bill sulked. "Do you think you could do better?"

"Drive," the Chinger said wearily. "Never let it be known that I have debated the merits of garbage dumping with a renegade human."

It was dusk before they reached a spot that suited Mgr's needs. A rocky patch in the hills, far from human habitation. While Bill was driving he had dismantled the driving robot and used some of its spare parts to build two complicated electronic devices. He plugged one in the cigar lighter socket and waved it around.

"What's that?" Bill asked.

"Detector detector for detecting detectors."

"What does it do?"

"I have always been nice to little Chingers and have helped old Chingers across the street—so what have I done to deserve you? Since you must know I am trying to find out if I can send my signal without the enemy knowing about it. And I can—so I plug this device in."

"What are you doing now?"

"Calling home obviously. There; the signal has gone out and we should get some results pretty soon. . . ."

It was sooner than that. His words were drowned out in the roar of landing jets as a hulking black craft dropped out of the sky and set down next to the truck. Mgr was on the ground in a single bound with Bill right behind him.

The airlock started to open and a microphone dropped out on a cord.

"Bgr I presume," Mgr enthused into the microphone.

A squad of combat marines dropped out of the bottom of the ship, blast rifles aimed. The door opened and a General with seven stars on his shoulders came smiling forth.

"Not Bgr," he said. "But General Saddam, head of Military Intelligence."

"Save me!" Bill shouted and ran behind the General to the safety of the blast rifles. "This enemy made me his prisoner—but I have found out his secret. His name is

Mgr and he is head of the CIA. Their top intelligence agency."

"Good work soldier. I suspected this Chinger from the very beginning, he was too easy to capture. And you have proven me right. My plans have worked perfectly!"

"No, General," Mgr sneered greenly. "My plans have worked perfectly. Harumph!"

Bill whipped the General's pistol from his holster and ground it into the General's neck as he jumped to put the officer's bulk between him and the gun-toting marines.

"Hey, guys!" he shouted. "If you shoot me you shoot the General, which would not look good on your records."

The marines stirred uneasily, some lowering their guns.

Their indecision was decided when with a great roar another black ship descended from the sky with its gun turrets swiveling. A blast of energy seared the ground before the troops and they hastily threw away their rifles.

"You can't do this!" the General roared, and tried to grab his pistol back from Bill who easily kept him at bay.

"Well done," Bgr said stepping out of the open part of the ship. "You were right about this one, Mgr."

"Thanks, Bgr."

Bgr made a sudden leap and seized the gun from Bill. "Un-harumph," he said.

"You almost broke my fingers off!"

"Tough. But for a moron you did a great job, Bill.

"Get into the ship. And you, General, right behind him. File for a pension because your retirement has just begun."

"You trapped me. This whole charade was just so you could get to me?"

"You bet our sweet patootie, General. Your side was getting too good. We figured out that someone really intelligent had gotten into the military and we couldn't put up with that. The only way we can keep winning the war is by letting the military chain of command stand. With the stupidest rising to the top."

A blast from the Chinger gun turret blew a hole through the other spacer and the marines fled for their lives. Mgr locked the General in chains as Bgr blasted them into the sky.

"You can drop me on some quiet planet, guys—okay?"

Bgr shook his head no. "Sorry, Bill, There's no discharge in the war. We need you in the Troopers. Maybe you too can be a General someday."

"Will I still get the Booze of the Month Club?"

"Sorry about that as well. It was but a figment of my imagination to tantalize you with."

"Then what do I get?"

"The rest of your R&R. All the officers are in the hospital with the sergeants taking care of them. We left behind a space freighter filled with every kind of alcoholic beverage known to mankind—as well as some unknown. All of your mates have imparted on a monumental binge and we know that they would like you to join them."

"Traitor!" the General hissed. "Your name will live in infamy!"

"I suppose it will," Bill sighed. "Though it won't if you don't tell them."

"Count on that," Mgr said.

"Well, in that case, you better pull out the stops. I don't want the party to go on too long without me."

Author's Note: On the island of Hawaii there is an active volcano that has been erupting for eight years. It produces 1600 metric tons of sulfur dioxide, and other chemicals, per day. There is a civilian hotel upwind from the fumaroles. And there is a Military Rest Camp downwind, washed by the clouds of VOG. How art doth mimic life. . . .

SCIENCE FICTION FROM
HARRY HARRISON

☐ 53975-3   THE JUPITER PLAGUE $2.95
                                           Canada $3.95

☐ 53967-2   A REBEL IN TIME $3.95
                                           Canada $4.95

☐ 53965-6   SKYFALL $3.95
                                           Canada $4.95

☐ 51941-8   THERE WON'T BE WAR $3.99
              Edited with Bruce McAllister   Canada $4.99

Buy them at your local bookstore or use this handy coupon:
Clip and mail this page with your order.

Publishers Book and Audio Mailing Service
P.O. Box 120159, Staten Island, NY 10312-0004

Please send me the book(s) I have checked above. I am enclosing $ _____
(Please add $1.50 for the first book, and $.50 for each additional book to cover postage and
handling. Send check or money order only — no CODs.)

Name _____

Address _____

City _____ State / Zip _____

Please allow six weeks for delivery. Prices subject to change without notice.

THE BEST IN
SCIENCE FICTION